# CRUISING FOR LOVE

## THE ESCAPE SERIES

### ANN OMASTA

# FREE BOOK!

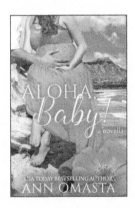

*Escape into the enchanting Hawaiian Islands by reading this heartwarming tale of friendship, love, and triumph after heartbreak.*

Free when you join Ann Omasta's VIP reader group. We value your privacy. Just visit annomasta.com and tell us where to send your free novella.

"*H*itting the cow in the road was *not* my fault!" I inform the others, making them burst into laughter yet again.

"Whose fault was it...the COW's???" This incredulous question comes from my best friend, Macy. She looks especially cute tonight because she has set her sights on her new co-worker, Kyle. When Kyle mentioned wanting to try the new Mexican restaurant in town, Macy had quickly thrown together this small group outing to ease her path into getting to know him better. I see them make eye contact, beaming at each other, and realize that my ridiculous hot mess of stories is serving as the ideal ice-breaker for them, which is likely exactly what Macy had intended when she brought up my less-than-stellar driving record.

"Well, yeah. I mean, what was it doing in the middle of the road?" It makes perfect sense to me, but they are still laughing at me. I chuckle, even though the hilarity is at my expense. I know it sounds crazy, but these odd situations just somehow seem to find me.

"Is the cow okay?" This concerned question comes as the

first words of the evening from our suddenly quiet friend, Jasmine. Jas is one of the most outlandishly fun people I know, but it takes her a while to warm up to strangers. Having the new faces from Macy's law office join us for dinner has evidently caused her shyness to flare up.

"The cow is fine," I reassure her. "My car on the other hand..." I let the sentence dangle, allowing the group to draw their own conclusions about my car's fate after tangling with a bovine. "I still go visit the cow occasionally," I add, "but I don't think she likes me."

"You're probably not her favorite person," Kyle confirms, earning a flirty eyelash flutter from Macy.

When the waiter drops off our second pitcher of frozen margaritas, Macy stands to pour refills of the slushy, lime deliciousness into everyone's glasses. She manages to give Kyle a lengthy peek at her ample cleavage as she bends to pour his drink. I can't help but chuckle as I watch his eyes nearly pop out of his head. If her intention with that maneuver had been to get his attention, she definitely succeeded.

"Tell them about your wreck with the Dr. Pepper truck, Ruthie." She encourages me to move on to the next car disaster story as she sits down and digs into the fresh basket of chips and salsa that have unobtrusively appeared at the table.

"Okay, but that one really wasn't my fault," I start, making them all laugh in anticipation of another of my ridiculous-but-true vehicle stories.

"They never are." Macy shakes her head at me.

As I proceed to tell them about the Dr. Pepper truck fiasco, which ended with my convertible being filled with exploding cans of hissing Dr. Pepper, I know we are being much too loud in the crowded restaurant. We are having fun, though, and I don't want to try to hold down the volume on our merriment.

Just then, one of the only people who could ruin my great mood walks in. She is already seated by the time she sees me, or I'm certain she would have slunk out of the restaurant like the man-stealing traitor that she is. My sister's ex-best-friend, Lizzie, and I make eye contact for the first time since she shattered Roxy's wedding day by stealing the groom. I narrow my eyes into a cool glare until she looks away.

I note that she isn't with Gary, the prick who had the audacity to dump Roxy by text message on their wedding day. Rumor has it that the man-stealer and the cheating jerk have broken up. *Karma can be a bitch,* I think to myself. Even though Roxy is giddily happy with her Hawaiian hunk, Kai, whom she met on her would-be honeymoon, I'm not quite ready to forgive and forget what Lizzie and Gary did to her. I might never be.

Lizzie's mother joins her, and I force my attention back to our table. The topic of conversation has now moved from my accident-prone driving skills to the plethora of jobs that I somehow manage to get fired from. *Great, now they all know that I'm vehicle AND job-challenged,* I think to myself. "She's always coming in late or not showing up at all," Macy tells the table. "Once she dropped an entire tray loaded with food. It's *never* her fault, though."

"It's not," I affirm, making the group laugh again as Macy pats my arm in a slightly condescending (but somehow still loving) way. I don't get offended by her teasing. It is all true, after all. My life is a series of complete disasters.

"She lost one job because she couldn't stand to leave Hawaii to come back to work," Macy shares with the group.

"It was HAWAII." I smile at them, lifting my shoulders as if that explains it all. *I might as well own it,* I decide. "Besides, it was totally worth losing that cocktail waitressing job to stay

3

in paradise a bit longer. I was able to attend Baggy's wedding while I was there. Baggy is my crazy grandmother," I clarify for Macy's co-workers. Deciding to go all in, I confide, "I missed my sister's wedding that same night, though, because I thought I saw Jason Momoa, and I went chasing after him."

Most of the others are shaking their heads in bewilderment, as if my life is the biggest train wreck they have ever encountered. "It wasn't him, but it *really* looked like him. I just *had* to follow him and find out."

It is quiet for a bit, so I add, "I guess I'm truly a jump-in-with-both-feet kind of gal...none of that dipping a toe in to test the water stuff for me." I smile at them, and most of them smile back.

As if the universe heard my bold declaration, a tall, well-dressed (if slightly slick looking) gentleman appears at our table. He hands me a business card, which I peer at warily. The card is made of thick black stock that feels surprisingly heavy in my hand. The gold block lettering says simply, "T.J. Stone, Producer."

I crane my neck up at him with a questioning look. Checking him out more closely, I find that he's wearing a tailored, dark suit. He is tan and has on more jewelry than any of the men from this area in the Midwestern section of the country would normally wear. I quickly decide he must be from California or New York City.

Speaking for the first time, he looks down at me and informs us, "I couldn't help overhearing your stories." I wonder if he expects an apology for our rowdiness. *He's not getting one,* I think to myself. *We were just having fun.* Instead of chastising us, he floors me by saying, "How would you like to be the world's next big reality television star?"

"*I*t will be fine, Mother." My attempts to appease the clearly disapproving woman are not working. I hold my cell phone away from my ear and roll my eyes toward the ceiling as she continues to detail the potential pitfalls with my plan.

She sounds like a broken record. Even after I set my cell on the counter––without bothering to put it on speaker-phone––I can hear key buzzwords. "Likely a scam...fall in the ocean...take advantage of you...contract terms...too naive for this Hollywood nonsense...steal your innocence."

I rub my temples in an attempt to stave off the impending migraine I can feel beginning to take root. As tempting as it is to hang up on my ever-negative parent, I know that some-where deep down she does have my best interests at heart. Her intentions likely come from a place of love, but conver-sations with her are often one-sided and nearly always emotionally draining.

Deciding I've had enough of her lecturing and choosing to take the easy way out, I pick up the phone and use one hand to muffle its microphone while I use my other fist to pound a fake knock on my counter. "I think someone's at my door," I announce to her.

The "hmph" she responds with lets me know that she isn't buying my ruse for a second. Determining that I'm in too far to back out now and opting to see it through, I add, "Talk soon. Bye." I utter the words quickly and hang up without waiting for her response, then I toss the phone on the counter, wanting to distance myself from her contrary juju.

Almost immediately, the phone begins jingling with an incoming call. "Give me a break, Mother," I say to my empty kitchen before picking the phone back up with the intention of sending her straight to voicemail. To my surprise, the display shows a smiling picture of my sister, Roxy.

"Aloha!" I answer excitedly. Roxy recently relocated to Hawaii, which makes it so she and I don't get to talk nearly as often as we used to, or as often as we would like.

Chuckling at my greeting, she responds, "Aloha, to you too."

"How are you?" I ask her, even though I can already tell by her relaxed and cheerful tone that she is happy. Kai, her sexy and sweet Hawaiian husband, seems to truly be her other half.

"I've never been better," she confirms before asking about me. "What's new in your world? Any strange car accidents this week?"

"Why would you ask me that?" I respond as if I am offended.

"You do have a knack for finding odd things to collide your car into," she reminds me gently before adding, "It's never your fault, though."

"I'm glad you realize that." We both chuckle at my tendency to deny blame, even though I am the only common denominator in all of the fiascos that seem to constantly shadow me.

Turning serious, she asks me, "You doing okay?" Having discovered her happily ever after ending, my sister now worries that I won't find mine.

"Actually, yes, I'm doing great. I have big news." She remains silent, waiting for me to spill it, so I take a deep breath before forging ahead. "I'm going on a reality television show that is set on a cruise ship and will be streamed on the internet." The words spill out of my mouth quickly. I brace myself for her reaction. Roxy has always been the practical sister, and I anticipate that her response will be similar to our mother's.

"What?" she asks me, clearly stunned. Without giving me a chance to respond, she surprises me by adding, "Wow! That's fantastic."

I'm thrilled and shocked by her extremely positive reaction. It is so much better than I would have ever imagined. Staying quiet, I wait for her to process what I have told her and begin lecturing me.

Rather than judging my spontaneity or questioning my sanity as I had fully expected, she continues to sound thrilled about my announcement as she asks me to tell her all about it.

Cringing slightly, I say, "I've already told you pretty much everything I know about it. I fly down to Florida on Friday to start shooting," I add, giving her the only other detail I gathered before signing on the proverbial dotted line.

"What an adventure! You're going to become America's Sweetheart," she proclaims, making me wonder if Kai has given her some kind of personality transplant. My fuddy-duddy, responsible sister would normally be in line right behind our mother to tell me what a ridiculous and hare-brained idea it is for me to agree to be on a reality television show without first going through the contract line-by-line with an attorney.

"Getting lei'd must be agreeing with you," I tease her with the double entendre, and she laughs so hard she actually snorts! I've never heard her be so carefree and giddily happy. It's sweet music to my ears.

Once our chuckling subsides, I tell her sincerely, "I'm so glad you found happiness."

"That's all I want for you," she responds, making me feel misty-eyed.

"Enough of this sappy stuff," I announce before adding, "Hang loose."

"You too. But not too loose," she adds as an afterthought, letting me know that the straight-laced sister I've always known and loved is still in there somewhere. Beaming from ear to ear, I press the button to end our call before heading to the hall closet to drag out my well-used burgundy suitcase. It's time to start packing for my adventure.

*I* crane my neck to stare up at the mammoth bow of
the ship in amazement. My intention had been to
play it cool in case any cameras were secretly recording my
arrival. So much for that plan...I'm openly gawking at the
enormous vessel. The fact that this steel behemoth floats
defies logic.

"I never dreamed it would be so big," I say to the porter
who is trailing behind me, wheeling the cart that is burdened
with my luggage. He smiles knowingly at me as if everyone
says this.

I ended up borrowing two additional suitcases from my
parents, so including the train case that holds my toiletries
and cosmetics, I have a total of four bags. I keep waffling
between being embarrassed that I brought so much to being
concerned that I won't have enough clothes. After all, I don't
want to be seen on air repeatedly wearing the same tired
outfit.

I see a family of four heading up the gangplank whose
porter isn't dragging as much luggage as the one helping me.
During the call I'd had with the show's PA, Jamie, she

mentioned that there would be 'regular' people on the ship, but that the show's participants would be kept separate from the tourists––for the most part.

Of course, as soon as I had hung up the phone from my conversation with Jamie, I came up with numerous questions that I should have asked her, but failed to think of during our brief chat. My detailed voicemails to her were left unanswered, and I didn't have a contact number for T.J., so I went with my best guesses as far as what to pack.

I stand there for a moment to enjoy the blazing heat of the intense sunshine beating down on my forehead and shoulders. My baggage helper stands patiently behind me as if he has nothing else to do all day. Deciding that he probably has plenty of other cruisers to assist and that I have come too far to back out now, I head toward the angled pedestrian bridge that the light-on-luggage family had just taken to board the ship.

A disconcerting thought enters my mind as I trudge up the walkway and the elegant interior of the ship begins to become visible. The producers sent me airline tickets and arranged a rush order on my very first passport, but I don't have an actual ticket for the cruise. The smiling attendant holds his hand out, clearly expecting me to hand him something to gain access to the ship.

I return his smile and lick my lips nervously. "Hi, umm, my name is Ruthie Rose." I had been hoping to see a flicker of recognition of my name as one of the people on the show, but his face maintains the vacant, sterile friendliness of a professional greeter.

We are silent for a bit before he nods briskly letting me know my awkward introduction was unnecessary. His eyes dart to his outstretched hand as he raises his brows slightly and says, "Ticket, please."

"About that," I start, uncertain how to continue. "You see,

umm." He peers skeptically at me over his reading glasses and I clear my throat nervously. "I'm on the television show that's going to be filming on the ship." Again, no recognition registers from him.

Deciding that this gatekeeper will not be the end of the line for my reality television career, I change tactics. I didn't come this far to not even make it aboard the ship. "Look," I say, trying to sound assertive, making the fake smile slide off his face only to be replaced with a weary stare, "don't you know who I am?" I cringe inwardly that those words have already slipped out of my mouth before filming has even started. Attempting to soften the edge of my crass question, I beam one of my most charming smiles at him. "Isn't there a list," I peek over the podium trying unsuccessfully to catch a glimpse of the papers in front of him, "of the stars of the television show that is going to be filming during this cruise?"

"There's no list, ma'am," he informs me sternly before adding, "and even if there was a list, you would still need a ticket to board this ship." I'm fairly certain he thinks I'm a total wackadoo.

I turn to my kindly luggage porter, who raises his shoulders as if to say he doesn't know what else to try. Several people are now lined up behind us, waiting patiently to gain access to their floating vacation home.

I'm quickly becoming embarrassed and frustrated-- mostly with myself for not asking Jamie about the ticket during our brief conversation. "Isn't there someone you can call?" I plead with the attendant.

He gives me a look that indicates his patience is wearing thin with me. Losing most of what is left of his professional courtesy, he rigidly informs me, "No ticket, no entry."

Completely at a loss for what to do, I can feel my face starting to crumple into tears. Even if I wanted to retreat down the gangplank, it is not wide enough to pass the group of ticketed passengers and porters now lined up behind me. They would all have to go back down to the sidewalk to give me a means of egress. I guess having an un-ticketed passenger attempt to board a cruise ship isn't a terribly common occurrence––at least not common enough to warrant setting up a second gangway.

The ticket agent is giving me the look of fear all men seem to acquire when dealing with a woman on the verge of tears. "Please," I try. "This is my big break. I'm supposed to become America's Sweetheart."

I see the slight smile the ticket agent tries to hide with an undoubtedly fake scratch of his nose. For some reason his smirk angers me. It's as if he can't believe that I might be on the cusp of a major breakthrough.

"I will make it," I vow to him. "You'll see...America will love me. The world will love me," I proclaim for some odd reason. I don't know what it is about this man, but something about him makes me want to prove my worth. Maybe it's because he controls the access to my future.

Dashing in like a savior, T.J. pops into the entryway. "Ruthie, darling!" he exclaims in a very 'Hollywood' tone. Air kissing my cheeks, he asks, "What is the holdup? Follow me."

I start to explain that my lack of a ticket is causing a problem, but T.J. turns to the man who has been holding up my progress, saying, "She is with me," and whisks past him with me in tow.

I rush through the metal detector and follow T.J. inside the sophisticated entrance lobby of the ship. For a moment, I wonder at the producer's ability to gain my entry onto the ship without a ticket, but I am soon distracted by my surroundings. Gazing in wonder at the pristine brass railings, shiny-mirrored elevators, and plush carpet, I am astounded by the luxurious decor of the enormous cruise ship.

My porter takes the luggage cart into one of the glass elevators and finger waves to me as T.J. and I head towards the stairs. My first thought is to hope he knows where to meet us, but then I relax, realizing that he does this every day and that it will all work out.

As we ascend one of the winding staircases, I listen to the music emanating from the grand piano and tell myself to take a deep, calming breath. The fiasco I encountered with embarking the ship is over now. Although I hadn't handled the situation nearly as smoothly as I would have liked to, at least the cameras aren't rolling yet.

Ordering myself to do a mental reset, I silently promise to remain calm and not let my emotions take over again. After all, my reactions during this show will be recorded for the whole world to see. I'd like to put my best foot forward.

*From now on, I'm going to be worthy of being an internet sensation*, I vow silently. Smiling happily, I whisper to myself, "You've got this," as I follow T.J. to my destiny.

## 4

*T*.J. leads me down a seemingly endless hallway before ushering me into a small cabin. "Hair and makeup," he announces as he swooshes me inside before exiting as quickly as he had appeared. I silently chastise myself for not asking a few of my many questions while I had the producer all to myself.

The room is long and narrow, but tiny. It does, at least, have a small balcony. Rather than a bed, it features an enormous lighted vanity with what seems like enough make-up and hair products to fill an entire shelf at Sephora.

I sit down on the white padded cushion of the dainty, metal chair. "Am I supposed to know what to do with all of this?" I wonder aloud, poking through the colorful compacts.

"Oh, no, Honey. That's what I'm here for." The voice startles me. I hadn't realized anyone had joined me in the room.

Using the lit mirror to stare at his reflection, I have to remind myself to close my mouth, which has fallen open of its own accord. The man who has joined me is absolutely gorgeous. His mocha skin and icy blue eyes make for an intriguing combination.

He walks over to me and lifts a lock of my long hair, which I just had highlighted with light-caramel colored streaks in honor of my television debut. "Hmm," he says noncommittally before ordering me to spin around in my seat so he can inspect me face-to-face. He's much closer than my personal space limit normally allows for people I don't know. In fact, he's so close that I can now see how impossibly perfect his complexion is. *Does the man not have any pores?*

I start to feel anxious under his intense scrutiny. After all, I have plenty of flaws. My hands feel clammy and dampness is starting to accumulate under my arms. It is an odd sensation because I almost never sweat.

Pulling back to stand to his full height, which has to be at least six feet, he raises a hand to his chin. He appears to be pondering what the verdict will be about his perusal of my face. I wonder if he is trying to think of a way to tell me he's not a miracle worker.

"I can work with this," he finally decides before beaming a smile at me and displaying his straight, blindingly white teeth.

Relief floods my system——warm and sweet. For some strange reason, this gorgeous stranger's approval had quickly become of the utmost importance to me. The rational side of my mind knows that one person's opinion of my physical attributes shouldn't matter so much, but my physiological response to his blatant examination of me is undeniable.

"First, you need to relax," he informs me as he uses an outstretched arm to indicate the long sofa stretched along the other wall of the cabin.

His announcement has the opposite effect. *Is this the proverbial casting couch on which so many stars over the years have had to perform sexual favors in exchange for fame? Or does he just want me to take a nap?* My musings causes a nervous bubble of laughter to escape from me.

As much as I want to be on this show and become the next big thing, I will not sleep with this man to get there. Even though he is super sexy and being with him would probably be beyond amazing, I'm not willing to sell myself out that way.

I stop in my tracks and turn back to him as he's ushering me to the sofa. "Look," I start, "I can't...I mean, I won't..." I stop, uncertain how to proceed with my denial of his advances.

He looks perplexed for a moment before giving me a knowing grin. He leans in to whisper in my ear, "You're not my type."

"Oh," I say awkwardly, somewhat hurt by his cutting honesty.

My expression must have betrayed my injured ego because he quickly amends his statement. "You're not my preferred gender," he reveals before leaning in to give me a quick peck on the cheek. His lips actually touch my skin, unlike T.J.'s earlier air kisses.

"Ohhh," I respond, comprehension dawning. For some reason, his news makes me feel much better.

"Now lie down and let me work my magic." His eyes sparkle as if he's testing me.

For some reason, my gut now trusts him, so I comply with his request. He is slender enough to sit down beside my prone body on the sofa. The next thing I know, a groan of pure bliss bursts out of me as he rubs away the tension I had apparently been holding in my neck and shoulders.

"You weren't kidding," I tell him after my lengthy, relaxing massage. "You have magic hands."

"So I'm told," he teases me, making me smile.

For some reason, I now feel completely at ease with this man. "I don't even know your name," I realize aloud.

"After what we just did on this couch? I'm shocked,

Ruthie!" His pronouncement indicates that he is already aware of my name. He smiles to let me know he's teasing.

"A random, handsome stranger bringing me to new heights of ecstasy on a casting couch...my dreams of fame are already coming true." He laughs at my silly joke, and I love the sound of it.

My limbs feel like limp noodles as I slither back over to the makeup chair. "My name is Sydney," he informs me, "but everyone who is anyone calls me Syd."

"I'm so glad to meet you, Syd," I say honestly before teasing, "I might let you have your way with me on a couch before knowing your name, but I would <u>not</u> let you touch my hair and makeup without it."

We both laugh loud enough to be heard out in the hallway, and I beam at him, certain that we are destined to be great friends.

## 5

"*T*urn around and look at me," he commands. "I need to get a good view of the palette I'm starting with."

Feeling a little nervous, I comply with his request.

He stoops down and takes his time, studying me closely. The tiniest frown lines appear on his forehead when something during his intense perusal of my features seems to displease him. Somehow the minute wrinkles manage to make him look even more handsome.

"What's wrong?" I ask him.

"Are you completely relaxed?" He answers my question with one of his own.

"Of course," I tell him. "Your magic hands just made me feel as pliable as a warm bowl of wax."

I had anticipated at least a grin from my response to his query. Instead, his brow furrows further. "I have some bad news for you," he finally divulges.

Feeling overly anxious about what it could be, I nod, indicating for him to go on. "Honey," he clasps one of my hands within his as if he is about ready to give me a death sentence. "You have RBF."

"I have what??" I ask him, feeling completely alarmed. *Is this some new form of cancer or some other dreaded disease that I've never heard of? How can he tell I have it just by looking at me?* Whatever it is, I can tell it's serious by his dire tone and mannerisms.

"Here, I'll show you." He spins me in the seat to face the mirror.

I gaze at my reflection, tilting my head from side to side trying to see what he is so concerned about. My eyes dart to him when he inhales sharply.

In response to my questioning look, he says, "You compensated as soon as I turned you around. Your face perked up immediately when you faced the mirror." Almost as an afterthought he adds, "You have no idea that you have it, do you? You've been lying to yourself all of this time."

Starting to get annoyed with this cryptic and worrisome discussion, I snap, "Oh, for heaven's sake, what in the world is RBF?"

"It's best if you see for yourself," he answers. "Turn away from the mirror and relax."

"That's easier said than done," I inform him as I attempt to un-scrunch my face, despite the concerns he has raised.

"Just relax," he says calmly as he gently squeezes my shoulders, rubbing his thumbs along the blades, which are now holding renewed tension--thanks to his mysterious acronym.

He bends down to peer into my face as he rubs. Once he's satisfied with my expression, he says, "Okay, now freeze. Don't move a muscle," he instructs me as he slowly turns me towards the mirror. "There, see it?" he asks, indicating my face. "That's one of the worst cases of resting bitch face that I have ever seen," he informs me.

"Resting bitch face?" I squeak, having never heard the term.

"See how your mouth points downward and your eyebrows look hostile?" I stare at the mirror, starting to see what he is talking about.

I begin to feel panicky about this new condition that I wasn't aware of, so I turn to Syd with pleading eyes. "What does this mean?" I ask him, unsure what to do.

"It just means that when you are in a relaxed state, your face makes you look like a total bitch." I recoil at the harshness of his words, so he softens the blow by adding, "It's no big deal, Honey. I've read that twenty percent of women suffer from it, and most of them have no idea, either. The problem is that people tend to naturally perk up their faces when they face a mirror or camera. We literally put our best face forward, but then we end up not knowing what we truly look like to others when our faces are relaxed."

His explanation makes sense, but it doesn't alleviate my concerns. "The cameras will be following me all of the time on this show. Am I supposed to try to keep a perpetual smile on my face, so I don't look like a total witch on television?"

"It's bitch," he reminds me before elbowing me lightly and chuckling to let me know he is teasing. "And no, you can't possibly smile all the time. Besides, you'd look like a weirdo."

"Agreed," I nod, "But what can I do? I want to be seen as the internet's Sweetheart, not the internet's angry Bitch-Face Queen." Even though I'm truly concerned, I can't help but chuckle along with him. Liking the sound of his laughter, I continue, "Is there a Bitch-Face Anonymous Club I can join?"

At this, he cackles and I join in, even though the comedy is at my expense. Once our laughter subsides, he helps alleviate my concerns. "You don't need a twelve-step program," he informs me before adding confidently, "That RBF doesn't stand a chance against me and my makeup kit."

I want to feel reassured by his words, but a mental image flashes into my mind of me going on television with a permanent, creepy make-up smile plastered to my face like the Joker from Batman.

"Oh Dear," Syd says upon seeing the concerned expression that I am unable to hide. "It looks like someone needs some beauty rest." He helps me stand and ushers me to an adjoining room that appears to be my cabin. I'm pleasantly surprised to see that my belongings have already been delivered, but it's a little disconcerting that my suitcases have been unpacked. I'm not sure how I feel about having had a stranger rifling through my personal things.

That concern is quickly overshadowed by Syd's next words. "Why don't you take a hot shower and have a quick catnap?" I like the sound of his suggestion until he adds, "You need your beauty rest before your wedding tonight."

I turn to him with wide eyes before he closes the door and latches the lock from his side. "My what?!?" I screech and pound on the door, jiggling the handle trying unsuccessfully to regain entry to the makeup room, but the other side of the door is completely silent.

## 6

*I* pace back and forth in my room before poking my head out into the hallway. It seems to stretch endlessly in both directions, with a plethora of closed doors. I have no idea where anyone else related to the show is staying.

After considering going to the ship's lobby and demanding to see T.J., I finally decide to take a few moments to calm down. Perhaps a shower is in order. After all, I have the grime of a half-day of travel on me. I'm not sure when filming will begin, but I'd rather at least be clean when I make my television debut. Trouncing out half-cocked and filthy to yell at the producers of the show would not make a terrific first impression.

I'll get this ridiculous wedding business straightened out once I am clean and presentable. They can't *make* me get married, right? I'm starting to wish I'd read that thick contract that was overnighted to me before I had blindly signed it.

As I let the steamy water in the barely-big-enough-for-one-person shower wash over me, I decide that I am in charge of me, no matter what that contract says. They probably want me to pitch a hissy fit about the surprise wedding. It would make for great television, but it would also make me look like a spoiled brat.

Instead, I will calmly tell them that the wedding is off. Perhaps the show can follow me and my intended groom as we go on a few dates and get to know each other? Or we could place the man they have chosen in a group of eligible bachelors to see if I choose the same one they have selected for me? That would make it a Bachelorette on the high seas kind of thing. There are plenty of ideas that will work without requiring a quickie wedding to someone I've never met.

By the time I emerge from the shower, I am calmed down and confident that I can talk some reason into the show's producers. Deciding that it has already been an exhausting and emotional day, I pull back the covers, intending to relax for a few minutes on the cool cotton sheets.

*I* must have fallen into a deep sleep because when I awaken to the sound of knocking on my adjoining door, the sun is setting over the horizon of the water. Deciding that whoever is on the other side can wait for a minute, I walk over to the sliding glass door to peer outside.

An expanse of blue water greets me. Surprised that I slept through our departure, I gaze out at the ocean. This is my first time on a ship of this size, and I'm relieved to see that we really are seaworthy, despite the significant tonnage the vessel must weigh.

Walking back to fling the door open, I'm pleased to see Syd, even though he has shocked me a couple of times

ANN OMASTA

already today with his flippant announcements. "Shouldn't they have beeped the horn or something when we left?" I ask him.

He smiles at my question. "They blasted the whistle when we embarked," he informs me before adding, "There was also a muster drill and bon voyage party on the pool deck."

"How did I miss all that?" I wonder aloud, truly perplexed.

"I looked in on you, but you looked so peaceful in your sleep that I told them to leave you alone."

"Isn't the safety drill mandatory?" I ask him, perplexed that I was able to skip out on something that seems so important, and still somewhat concerned about the ship's seaworthiness.

"It's amazing the clout the show has already," he informs me. "I let them know I would take care of you, and I will, Honey." He points to my closet. "Your life vest is in there. If the alarm sounds, follow the glowing arrows on the carpet to our lifeboat. I won't let you drown."

For some reason his words reassure me, even though I barely know the man. All thoughts of safety are quickly washed away as I follow him into the adjoining room. A rolling cart of gorgeous gowns has been wheeled in.

"Oh my!" Unable to stop myself, I walk over and begin looking through them. Each one is more fabulous than the last, and I squeal with delight over them.

"I'm glad you approve of our dress selections for you," the words come from T.J. He and Jamie have quietly entered the room from the hallway.

I turn to them, intending to hold my ground. "They are beautiful," I say honestly, before adding, "but I am not getting married tonight."

T.J. raises his eyebrows slightly as if my words amuse him. "Is that so?" He almost sounds like he's mocking me. "Your contract says otherwise."

"I don't care," I lift my chin in defiance. "I refuse to marry someone I don't know. There are other ways we can make the show work. I have plenty of ideas." Before I can begin to explain any of my thoughts, T.J. holds up a hand to stop me.

"Have it your way," he replies, making me wonder how I won him over so easily. I had thought I would have to do some major sweet-talking and negotiating. Then he reveals what he really means. "We'll find someone else to be on the show...someone who is grateful for the chance to win the $250,000 grand prize."

My mouth falls open. I assumed I would get paid something for my appearances on the show, but being an unknown, I thought most of my reimbursement would come from advertisements and special guest appearances once I became a household name. A quarter of a million dollars is beyond my wildest dreams. That amount of money could set me up for a long time. All of a sudden, the quickie wedding, while still outrageous, doesn't seem quite as preposterous.

Striking while the iron is hot, T.J. continues, "I'm sure there are plenty of young women who would love to take your place on the show and become famous. You are welcome to disembark the ship and fly home at our next port. This will be at your own expense, of course."

He smiles, but it's the smile of a crocodile, and I know I won't like whatever is coming next. "Oh," he starts like he has just thought of it, "you'll need to reimburse us the money for your tickets for the plane ride here and the cruise. Jamie," he turns to the woman standing slightly behind him, "find out how much Ruthie will owe us for her tickets, please."

"Sure," the woman nods, already pulling out her smartphone to do the needed research.

"We'll let you know the damages," T.J. informs me briskly as he turns to usher Jamie out of the room with him.

I don't need to hear the answer to know that it's more

than I can afford. I'm doubting my decision to trust this slick producer, but I'm in too deep to turn back now. "Wait," I say, making the crocodile turn and grin at me like I am fresh prey that has just slithered into his swamp.

## 7

The croc and his assistant made a quick exit after assuring me that everything would be just fine. I turn to Syd, the only person on this ship that I trust at all, for advice.

"What should I do?" I ask him desperately.

"It's the chance to win a lot of money," he says rationally. At my nod, he continues, "And who knows, maybe it will be a true love connection."

I smile at him as he rolls my hair around the hot curling wand. I know that he's trying to be kind, but I need to talk to someone who has my best interests at heart...like my sister, Roxy, or my crazy grandma, Baggy.

Unfortunately, whoever unpacked my belongings had confiscated my cell phone. This discovery sent me into a minor panic attack over the picture I keep with me to look at every night before bed, but I found it still tucked away in the pocket of my suitcase. Immense relief flooded me when I realized it hadn't been taken, or likely even seen. I don't want to share that particular secret with the show's viewing audience, yet I still hadn't been willing to leave home without the photograph.

Before my nap, I had tried unsuccessfully to make a call from the desk phone in my room. Apparently, part of the 'fun' of this show is cutting us off from communicating with our loved ones.

Turning to Syd, I ask, "Is this crazy?"

"Yes, absolutely," he answers honestly before adding, "but that's okay."

Wondering what he means, I turn to look directly at him rather than his reflection in the mirror. He squats down so he can look at me eye-to-eye. "Think how much you have to gain from this, Honey. You might become famous, you might win a ton of cash, and I know you think it's crazy, but you just might find the man of your dreams."

I nod, acknowledging that his points are valid, but still uncertain about this whole arranged marriage thing. "And what do you have to lose?" he asks me logically. "Do you have a man waiting for you at home?"

"No," I admit, before adding, "but what if I can't stand the guy they've chosen for me?"

"So what?" he asks, flooring me.

"I'll be married to him," I remind Syd, wondering if he's gone dense.

"So, get an annulment or divorce him after the show. Honestly, it would probably make for better television if you didn't like each other––at least at first."

I ponder his words. They make a lot of sense. I had been looking at this wedding like it was supposed to be my 'happily ever after' ending. There is a slight, miniscule chance that it will be, but even if it's not, it isn't the end of the world. I hadn't looked at it like that before.

"So, I get a tropical vacation, I have a good chance of becoming famous, I might win loads of cash, and it's possible that I could meet the man of my dreams." I beam a smile at Syd as the reality of my good fortune begins to settle in once more. I had let the wedding thing throw me for a loop, but now my initial enthusiasm about being on the show is beginning to return.

"Now you're talking." Syd encourages me.

"And worst case scenario is that it ends up not being a good match, and I get a divorce."

"Which happens to half of all marriages anyway," Syd puts in. "Actually, you might have better odds than most of being happy together because I heard they ran extensive profiles on each of you to determine your best match."

This is news to me. I remember filling out and returning a personality profile in the packet from Jamie, but I hadn't realized it was being used to find me a suitable partner. "Who knows," I decide, starting to feel hopeful, "maybe this will work."

"Maybe," Syd agrees before suggesting enthusiastically, "Now, let's pick out your wedding gown!"

"$\mathcal{N}$ope," Syd says firmly to the fifth dress.

They have all been stunning, and I am beginning to wonder if he will like any of them. It takes significant effort for me to get into each one, only to have him make a snap and negative decision about it at the first glimpse of it on me. I select another gown from the rack and trudge back through the adjoining door to my room to change.

This one fits like a glove. I can feel how perfect it is before I even glance at the mirror. Feeling nervous that Syd will shoot it down without giving it a fair shot, I open the door.

"Hmm." He lifts a hand to his chin as he studies me. "Let me zip you up all the way." He turns me so he can reach the back. This is farther than any of the previous gowns have gotten with him, and I begin to feel excited that this might truly be the one.

I turn back to face him, and he stands back so I can see the mirror. "Wow," both of us say in unison before beaming at each other.

"I think we've found the one," he reveals. "Who cares what the groom is like when you have a gown like that?" I'm pretty sure he's joking, but the dress is truly beyond gorgeous. "Now get out of it," he orders me. "I'll get rid of the others," he flips a hand toward the dress rack as if they are completely unworthy, "then we can get to work on your makeup. We can't have you getting married with RBF." He smiles to let me know he's teasing about that last part.

Once I return in the plush creamy colored robe I discovered in my room, Syd carefully hangs and fusses over the dress that will be my wedding gown. I am pleased to find he has placed undergarments and shoes near the dressing table. Walking over to try one of the shoes, he snaps at me before I can slide it on my foot. "You are not even thinking about putting a bare foot into those shoes, are you, Darling?"

"Of course not," I respond, quickly changing my mind. Deciding that I don't know how long I'll be forced to stand around in them, I ask, "Shouldn't I make sure they fit?"

Syd seems completely taken aback and offended by my question. "They'll fit," he replies firmly and rather cockily, and that is the end of that discussion.

Seeing no choice but to take his word for it, I walk back over and plop into the makeup chair. Syd has me turn to face him. "No peeking at the work in process. You'll get the big reveal once I've made you dazzling from head to toe."

He is not kidding about that. After rubbing the most luxurious and delectably scented cream onto my hands and feet, he polishes my nails a shimmering pale pink. Opting to trust him, I relax and let him work to combat my RBF.

He tweezes, powders, rouges, curls, buffs, and puffs me for what seems like an inordinate amount of time. After eventually proclaiming me to be "finis," he orders me to the adjoining room to get dressed.

The white, lacy panties and strapless bra are much sexier than the undergarments I normally wear, but I don them without complaint. It is my wedding day, after all. Just the thought of this makes my stomach churn with nerves. *Am I making a ginormous mistake? How can I marry someone I haven't ever even laid eyes on?*

Someone knocks on the hallway door, yelling, "Fifteen minutes!" The announcement startles me out of my rumination, and I quickly step into the beaded gown. Squeezing my arms down to hold the dress in place, I return to Syd's side to have him zip me into it.

He busies himself situating the dress, pinning my tiara veil into place, and giving my tresses a final spray. Bringing my shoes over and setting them in front of me, he steadies me as I slip my feet into them. "Perfect," I admit, and he gives me a knowing grin.

"Never had any doubt," he says rather arrogantly before softening it with, "I'm very good at my job." He bends down to kiss me sweetly on the cheek before excitedly proclaiming, "Now for the best part!"

After punching some numbers into the room's squatty safe, he stands to present me with a slender box. Flipping it open dramatically, he says "Ta-da!"

My breath catches in surprise. "Is that thing real?" I ask, gazing at the gorgeous necklace. It features a large heart-shaped sapphire in the middle of numerous sparkling diamonds.

He nods in answer before adding, "Please don't throw it into the ocean like that batty old bitty on the movie Titanic."

"I would never," I reassure him as he gently clasps the beautiful bauble around my neck.

"Gorgeous," he proclaims as he stands back to get a good look at me. "Okay, the dress is something new, the necklace is borrowed and blue..." He is making check marks in the air with his finger. "We just need something old." His eyes travel around the room as he taps his chin in thought.

I am touched that he is trying so hard to make my

wedding perfect––all the way down to complying with an old adage that is more than likely just a silly wives' tale.

Deciding to join in the fun, I announce, "I have the perfect thing." Swishing into my room, I search my drawers until I find it. Returning to Syd, I hold up Baggy's delicate handker-chief. "It's my grandmother's," I tell him. "She gave it to me for good luck." I don't bother to tell him that knowing Baggy, it's probably something she picked up at a Dollar Store rather than a family heirloom.

"Perfect," he decides, nodding, before ushering me over to the bathroom door. He swishes the door open dramatically, and I am presented with a full-length mirror.

"Wow!" I am stunned by the first look at my reflection. Syd has subtly accentuated my features and somehow made my skin appear flawless. I turn my head from side to side, gazing at my likeness. This is by far the best I have ever looked, and I am incredibly grateful to him. "I'm a beautiful bride," I gush.

"Indeed you are," Syd confirms, smiling warmly. When my eyes start to mist, threatening to spill tears, he changes his tune quickly. "No crying and messing up my masterpiece," he orders firmly. At my nod of understanding, he adds, "Now, let's go meet your groom."

## 9

*My* nerves kick in fully as we take the elevator up to the pool deck. *What is my groom-to-be like? Will I have a chance to talk to him before the ceremony? What if I can't stand him? What if he can't stand me?*

"I feel like a herd of butterflies have been set free in my stomach," I confide to Syd.

"A *herd* of butterflies?" he grins at me, and I raise my shoulders, smiling back. Seeming to catch on that I need to focus on something innocuous, he decides, "I bet it's a gaggle of butterflies."

"A gaggle?" I shake my head. "That's geese." Deciding to throw out some more silly guesses, I suggest, "A pride? A litter? A pack? A school?"

He is shaking his head to shoot down each of my suggestions. Once we emerge from the elevator, he pulls out his cell phone––apparently his hasn't been confiscated. After asking his voice recognition personal assistant what a group of butterflies is called, he turns to me and announces excitedly, "It's a flutter!"

Several people turn to give us strange looks at his odd

declaration, but neither of us care. "A flutter of butterflies makes perfect sense, and that's exactly what it feels like in my tummy," I tell him.

We are shuffled over to a waiting area behind a double set of doors, which an arrow sign indicates lead out to the pool. For the first time, I see a camera recording all of the action. T.J. and Jamie appear suddenly. She works to hide a wireless microphone pack on my back as T.J. asks, "All ready, dear?"

"As ready as I'll ever be." I try to smile at the camera, despite my nerves.

"Pretend they're not even here," T.J. instructs me, indicating the cameraman, before swishing away.

Nodding, I attempt to dry my sweaty palms on the handkerchief Baggy has given me. I turn to tell Syd it is a good thing I have it, but he is gone. The small crowd gathered around me is filled with strangers, and I already miss him immensely. Even though I've only known him part of a day, I need a familiar and friendly face nearby right now.

I don't have too long to worry about it because the double doors are pulled open and the wedding march begins playing. I am handed a sweet-smelling bouquet of fresh peonies––my favorite flower––before being ushered forward.

I never envisioned myself walking down the aisle alone. Knowing that my family will be watching this when it airs, I wonder if my father will feel cheated at not having been permitted to guide me along the path to this major rite of passage.

Emerging from the covered area, the first thing that catches my eye is the gorgeous sunset over the water. The sky is filled with an amazing array of oranges and reds. The producers have planned the timing of the ceremony perfectly because the lighting is amazing.

Following the white runway, I turn from side to side and

notice for the first time that there are brides on either side of the ship. They are both beautiful--one with platinum blond hair, the other with long red waves. Three walkways head towards the pool and three men in black tuxes await us near the edge of it. I am surprised to see the other couples, but am pleased to have been placed in the middle. *That has to be a good sign, right?*

Speaking of good signs, the man fidgeting nervously in the middle of the grooms appears to be tall, dark, and handsome from this distance. I hope that holds true as we get closer to each other. Excited, I pick up the pace, wanting to get a good look at him.

"Cut!" The sharp word interrupts the reverie of the moment.

T.J. appears from nowhere. "Ruthie, darling, you have to stay even with the other brides." He sweeps his hands out in both directions, indicating how far ahead of the other two I am.

Both of the other ladies are giving me disgusted glares, as if I have just ruined their big moment. "Oh, ummm, sorry," I stammer.

"Let's try this again, sloooowly." T.J. gives me a patronizing smile before shuffling me back to the entrance doors.

I am turned and fluffed by a pointy-nosed lady holding a clipboard, then the music restarts, indicating it is time for me to walk down the aisle--again.

This time, I nervously watch the brides on either side of me to make sure I am proceeding at the proper pace. I am so busy monitoring their progress that I almost forget to check out my husband-to-be. Once he captures my attention, I am unable to look away. I have definitely hit the jackpot in the never-seen-before groom department.

He is at least six inches taller than me, and if the way his tux tightly hugs his torso is any indication, he has a magnificent body. The best part about him is his piercing green eyes that are gazing at me with a mixture of relief and lust. It is obvious that he likes what he sees, and I feel exactly the same way.

I am so busy looking at him that I fail to hold up my gown as I'm walking up the two steps to the pool platform where he and the other grooms are waiting. On the second step, the front of my high-heel catches in the hem of my dress and I stumble forward. My quick-reacting groom saves me from falling all the way to the ground by catching my arm to steady me.

Our eyes lock as he helps me regain my balance, and I feel a definite spark of attraction zing between us.

"Cut!" The sharp voice interrupts the moment again. "Let's try that one more time without anyone tripping over her own feet."

The other two brides and I are led back to the midpoint of each of our white paths. I can feel the woman on the right shooting eye daggers at me. I turn to mouth the word "Sorry" to her, but she looks angrily away before I have a chance. She has gads of blazing red curls that trail down her back, and I'm sensing that she has a fiery temper to match her locks. I fear that my clumsiness has already made me an enemy of hers.

Silently vowing to be more careful, I slowly and steadily march up the aisle for the third time. This time, when I get close enough, Mr. Handsome reaches out a hand to assist me up the steps. I smile at him in thanks, thinking that maybe––just maybe––he could be my knight in shining armor.

I can feel the bouquet of colorful peonies shaking uncontrollably in my hands as I turn to face him. The silver ribbons dangling from it are visibly swaying.

"Cut!" The now-familiar, but still annoying voice breaks in. "She's shaking like a leaf." The director points at me and I hear a loud huff of frustration emit from the red-haired bride. "Plus, she's managed to get her dress all twisted. Can someone fix her, please?" he yells to the myriad of stagehands and assistants who have unobtrusively moved in behind the cameras.

I can feel my cheeks burning hot with embarrassment as my clipboard-carrying helper dashes in to take the bouquet and straighten the train of my gown. "Sorry," I mutter, but she ignores me.

I'm not sure why I'm the only one who seems to be having any troubles. The other two brides have their own assistants who whisk their bouquets out of the way and re-fluff them, but apparently I'm the only one who *needed* the break. It makes me wonder what would happen if this had been a real-time wedding, rather than a made-for-television one. *Would I have fallen or gotten married with my dress a twisted mess? How do the other two make it looks so easy and natural?*

Trying not to worry too much about it, I focus on my groom after the director calls for "Action!" We each repeat what the Captain of the ship guides us to say. I'm not a big fan of the three-for-one vows, having always thought that my wedding would be my own special day, but I try not to let that ruin the monumental moment.

When it comes time to insert our names, the Captain turns to each of us. When it's my turn he instructs me, "I, Ruth, take you, Cameron, to be my lawfully wedded husband." I bristle at his use of the name Ruth and utilize my preferred moniker, Ruthie, when I repeat it back. I'm pleased to hear my almost-husband's name, though. I've always liked the name Cameron and wonder if he goes by Cam. It's a sexy name that suits him well.

A stagehand appears at the appropriate moment to hand us the wedding bands. Glancing down as we exchange them, I'm pleased to see simple, elegant platinum rings.

The rest of the ceremony goes by in a blur and before I know it, the Captain indicates it is time for the grooms to kiss the brides. As Cam pulls me into his arms, I sidle closer and tip my head back, awaiting our momentous first kiss to seal the deal on this marriage.

Cam moistens his lips with a flick of his tongue before pressing them to mine. I close my eyes, wanting to remember this life-altering moment forever. When he opens his lips slightly to deepen the kiss, I follow suit. Our tongues brush against each other tentatively, and it feels glorious––like the perfect first kiss.

Forgetting everything except our mouths, I allow a groan of happiness to escape. Apparently viewing my approving sound as permission for more, Cam deepens the kiss. Before I have time to react, his tongue fully invades my mouth, forcefully probing in further––nearly gagging me. I yank my head back instinctively, trying to end the onslaught, but his hand on the back of my neck effectively holds me in place. I try not to be overly obvious in my distaste, ever mindful of the camera on the step below us recording every move we make––probably in close-up, high definition.

Finally, I am able to tip back and far enough away from him to end the kiss. Cam smiles at me before saying, "Wow!"

"Yeah, wow," I reply, quite certain that I don't mean it in the same way he does.

He helps me stand back up straight, and I realize that the other two couples are gawking at us. Evidently our first kiss lasted longer than either of theirs had.

The Captain clears his throat before announcing, "I now present to you, Mr. and Mrs. Paul Thomas," indicating the bride with the whitish blonde hair and her new husband. Turning to us, he says, "Mr. and Mrs. Cameron Belchmeister."

"What?!?" I blurt as he turns to the couple with the

redheaded bride. "My last name is now Belchmeister?" I screech without thinking. I wonder why they don't pronounce the "ch" with a hard "k" sound so at least the name wouldn't sound like the King of the burpers.

My new husband is looking at me as if he can't imagine what my problem could possibly be with his surname. The bride whose announcement has been disrupted by my outburst is glaring at me as if she wishes I would keel over on the spot. The director is holding a palm to his forehead and shaking his head back and forth as if he suddenly has a piercing headache.

At least he hasn't called "Cut!" again on my account. Deciding to try to smooth things over, I add quietly. "I was planning to keep my last name, Rose."

The Captain turns to announce the final couple with a look of exasperation evident on his face. I don't even register the names because of the blood rushing in my ears. I so wanted to make a good first impression with my television debut, yet had somehow managed to make a complete ass of myself at my own wedding. Hopefully, they will cut out the embarrassing parts of the ceremony in editing.

After the final couple is presented, applause erupts on the deck above us. For the first time, I realize a crowd of actual passengers on this cruise has gathered at the railings to watch our weddings. Feeling silly about my numerous faux pas, but grateful for their warm reception, I wave timidly up at them.

With perfect timing, "At Last" by Etta James begins playing over some hidden speaker system. My new husband takes my hand and guides me to a makeshift dance floor on the pool deck. We dance slowly, and I lean my head against his shoulder, enjoying the feeling of being held in his embrace.

As we dance, I decide that everything can still turn out

okay. I'll keep my last name and apologize to the other girls for my klutziness during our wedding. I'll be more careful going forward, and I *will* win over the viewing audience.

That horrible kiss is still weighing somewhat heavily on my mind, but that can be fixed, right? I can train Cam on what I like and don't like. It will be fun to practice, and I'll be careful to approach the subject sensitively, so as not to hurt his feelings along the way.

When the music changes to a more upbeat song, Cam swings me around, proving that he does have some smooth moves. We are laughing, swaying to the music, and having a grand time. As the song comes to a rousing end, Cam lifts his arm to twirl me around. I gracefully spin around a couple of times before knocking into the red haired bride who is chatting with the Captain and manage to knock them both into the pool.

As I stand at the pool's edge, still dry and gorgeous, the furious, dripping wet bride splutters to the surface. If I had any doubt before, I'm certain that she hates me now. The Captain glares up at me as he retrieves his waterlogged hat and returns it to his nearly-bald head.

I'm horrified by this entire turn of events. As much as I'd love to blame the rocking of the ship, I fear it's just my clumsiness that has caused this catastrophe. Wanting to do anything I can to help, I reach a hand down to the soaked bride. "I'm so sorry! Here, let me help you."

I only have an instant to see the gleam in her eye as she accepts my offered hand, just before yanking me into the pool with her. I break the surface, shocked that she would purposely dunk me, when what I had done had clearly been an accident. Taking a moment to calm down, I decide to make the best of a rotten situation.

The other bride is still glaring at me. Obviously, getting even hadn't lessened her anger. I look at the black streaks trailing from her eyes and realize that I must look just as ridiculous. Unable to stop myself, a snort of laughter bubbles out of me.

Her eyes blaze at me for a moment, but then I see a transition in her. "You are an absolute hot mess," she finally says as she erupts with her own laughter.

"So I'm told," I admit, as my new husband proves he's up for anything by jumping into the pool in his tux.

Before long, all of the brides and grooms are in the water and the Captain has scurried out to dry off. Cam suggests we water wrestle and lifts me onto his shoulders. The other couples follow suit and we each try to knock the other couples down. We laugh and play like kids.

Out of the corner of my eye, I see the director swiping a hand over his face, but I notice he keeps the cameras rolling. I'm guessing this isn't at all how he planned for things to go, but it should at least make for interesting television.

IO

*A*fter a good amount of playing in the pool, we are instructed to return to our rooms to get ready for dinner with the Captain. This announcement makes me somewhat nervous because I'm fairly certain I'm not his favorite person, after having unceremoniously dumped him in the pool.

Jamie, the PA, escorts me to my room. I notice the others don't get a private guide. It makes me wonder if the show's producers think I can't find my room on my own or if they fear I'll get in trouble along the way if left to my own devices. Either way, I try to chat with the woman, but she merely nods or shakes her head in answer to my questions. Once we reach the threshold of my room, she ushers me in and shuts the door with her on the other side.

Dying to dish about all that has happened, I quickly remove my wet gown, don the comfy, cotton robe, and try the door to the adjoining make-up room. I'm pleased to find it unlocked. Syd is sitting on the sofa, so I scurry over to join him.

He bugs his eyes out at my appearance. "What happened

to my masterpiece?" His voice sounds screechy with disapproval.

I proceed to fill him in on what has happened since I left him. "Never a dull moment with you, Girl." He chuckles as I describe the wet ending to our ceremony. Turning somewhat serious, he adds, "It looks like you hit the jackpot in the arranged marriage department. I peeked at your groom, even though they told me to come straight back here. He is cuuu-uute." He drags the word out and emphasizes the last part by lightly shoving my shoulder.

Nodding in agreement with his assessment of tall, dark, and handsome Cam, I give him a sad smile before adding, "Just one problem, though."

Syd's eyes widen at the prospect of learning some major gossip. "Spill," he orders me.

When I reveal the truth about our horrid wedding kiss that turned out to be by far the worst kiss of my entire life, Syd has the audacity to laugh. "It's not funny," I pout. "It was like my mouth was under attack by his probing tongue."

This description makes him cackle even harder. "Oh Honey," he tells me, "You can train him. Kissing is an art. Maybe he just needs a good teacher."

Hoping that he's right and that I'll be able to tactfully broach the subject without hurting Cam's feelings, I nod. "Oh, and I haven't told you his last name." After a dramatic pause during which Syd raises his perfectly groomed eyebrows in anticipation, I close my eyes before saying, "Belchmeister."

Syd audibly sucks in air, gasping at this revelation and patting his chest with one palm as if I've given him heart palpitations. "That just won't do," he decides firmly, shaking his head, appalled.

"I let them know that I'll be keeping my last name," I inform him.

"Good call. Maybe he should take your last name. Belch-meister..." He visibly shudders after saying the name aloud. "Well, here's hoping Ole' Belchmeister bangs better than he kisses, huh?"

Giving him an odd look, I say, "We're a long way from finding that out. I just met the man."

"And married him," Syd interjects.

"Yeah, but nobody could expect me to sleep with him right away. That's gross." I scrunch my face up at the thought.

"Hmm." Syd nods noncommittally, making me wonder what he knows. "Let's make you gorgeous for dinner," he changes the subject suddenly.

I decide not to worry about the whole sleeping together thing. Married or not, they can't make me do anything like that against my wishes. After promising to be back in 'two shakes of a lamb's tail,' which makes Syd look at me like I've grown an actual lamb's tail, I head over to my side of the adjoining rooms to shower off the chlorine from my unplanned post-wedding plunge in the pool.

## 11

*A*s promised, Syd makes me beautiful once more. He has selected an emerald green, beaded full-length gown that hugs my waist and somehow makes me look like I have actual curves. He returns the sapphire and diamond necklace I wore during the wedding to the room's safe and emerges with a stunning emerald choker and matching earrings.

"Wow!" I gush as he helps me put on the jewelry.

"One of the many perks of being on television," he reminds me.

"Me likey," I joke with him, making him smile at my reflection. I take a good look at his perfectly straight, brilliantly white teeth. The man is physically stunning, and it makes me wonder if he has aspirations of being in front of the camera, rather than behind the scenes.

When I try to ask him, he shoos me away, indicating that I'm going to be more than fashionably late for dinner if I don't get a move on.

Jamie is waiting just outside the door when I emerge. She looks at her wristwatch impatiently, before tipping her head indicating I should follow her. I scurry to keep up, but my tight dress and high heels aren't conducive to long strides.

"I noticed your watch," I say to the woman in an attempt to draw her into a conversation as we ride the elevator. When she doesn't acknowledge me, I continue, "Cell phones have all but replaced the classic wristwatch nowadays, huh?" I try again.

The woman gazes at the lit numbers indicating the floor changes without responding to my attempt at chitchat, so I give up. Turning to face the glass at the back of the elevator, I audibly gasp as we are lowered to the main deck of the ship. The marble floor, enormous crystal chandelier, and brass trim are all pristine and shiny. I feel like I am on a modern-day version of the Titanic. I just hope we aren't headed for a similar fate.

Jamie leads me into the grand dining hall. The massive room is empty, except for a large round table where the captain of the ship and the other participants in today's wedding are waiting. I'm distressed to find that I am the last one to arrive. I was hoping to stay a little more low-key for a while, since I had been the cause of today's wedding fiasco.

"Sorry I'm late," I huff as I plop into the vacant chair next to Cam. I'm out of breath from hurrying.

Cam leans over to give me a sweet kiss on the cheek, which helps calm my jittery nerves significantly, until the Captain sneers, "Well, I guess we can *finally* get started."

I am tempted to give him a snippy response, but I suppose he has every right to be annoyed with me. Besides, I am fairly certain that the gorgeous orange hibiscus centerpiece in our table hides several tiny video cameras.

The waiters zoom in to get our drink orders and deliver our clam chowder crocks and Caesar salads. The table falls into an awkward silence, so I attempt to fill in the void.

"Where is everyone else?" I ask the table at large, sweeping my hand out to indicate the empty dining hall.

Cam leans in to tell me the regular cruise passengers had a dinner seating earlier in the evening. I'm guessing by the way he whispers his answer that this topic was discussed prior to my arrival.

Silence prevails once more. For some reason, my diarrhea of the mouth kicks in when I'm nervous. Apparently, the lack of conversation at our table makes me anxious because I turn to the staid Captain and ask, "Has anyone ever told you that you look like Captain Stubing?"

It's a dated reference from an old show called 'The Love Boat.' Baggy used to love watching reruns of it whenever Roxy and I stayed with her. I can tell by the way he is glaring at me that he is familiar with the character.

The blank stares I am receiving from the rest of the table indicate that no one else has ever heard of the show. I wish they had because they would easily see that he truly is the actor's doppelganger.

"No," he says firmly, effectively putting an end to that topic. I'm pretty sure he's lying, but I'm sure as heck not going to call him out on it.

"Bellamy," the captain turns to the redheaded bride, smoothly shifting the conversation away from me. "You look absolutely ravishing this evening."

The woman beams at his praise before narrowing her eyes in my direction as if to say 'Bellamy 1, Ruthie 0.' There is no denying the accuracy of his statement. Her silvery gown looks glamorous and elegant. The color of her deep red hair almost looks burgundy in the glowing light of the dining room. The effect is absolutely striking against the shiny dress. Looking at the perfect, luxurious waves tumbling down past her shoulders, I wonder about her version of Syd.

He or she must be über talented, just like my wonderful stylist.

I decide to take the high road by smiling kindly at her-- after all, she has legitimate reasons for not being overly fond of me. It doesn't stop me from hoping that I'll be able to win her over. She quickly glances away as if she's unwilling to accept the idea that I might actually be a decent human being.

The captain is openly admiring Bellamy, which makes her new husband shift uncomfortably in his seat. Never taking his eyes from Bellamy, the captain gushes, "You're a lucky man, Joshua."

Josh is cute in a boy-next-door kind of way. His golden blond hair swooshing down towards his blue eyes makes a good match with his long, lean frame. When we were playing in the pool earlier, I noticed he has a dimple that pops out when he smiles, so that is an added bonus.

Right now, he's looking down at his soup tureen and shaking his foot violently enough that the water glasses are jittering like a T-Rex is heading our way. It is obvious the captain's overt attention aimed at his new wife is making him uncomfortable. He likely doesn't want to say anything for fear of causing a scene that will play out on television. The situation makes me feel bad for him and my initial distaste for Stubing--as I am now rebelliously (but silently) calling the stuffy captain--is growing exponentially.

Finally forcing himself to break his enamored gaze away from Bellamy, Stubing turns to the blonde bride. "You look gorgeous as well, Tiffany." Both the way he says it as an afterthought and how he purposely omits me from receiving any compliments totally irk me, but I try not to show it. Tiffany clearly holds no ill will about being second choice because she bubbles with high-pitched laughter.

Swooping in to save the day like a true hero, Cam lifts his

glass for a toast. "To all *three* beautiful brides." He pauses for added effect before adding, "We are some lucky bastards to have gotten to marry them."

He has effectively broken the ice as we all laugh and clink our crystal champagne glasses with the people on either side of us. I'm even more grateful for Cam as he leans over to whisper in my ear, "You are by far the most beautiful." His sweet words make my cheeks feel warm as I decide I kind of like having a husband on my side. When he reaches over to clasp my hand in his much larger one, I don't object.

*T*hroughout the course of our dinner, I begin to see the roles that we have been cast to play in the show. Reality television or not, I'm confident the producers were looking for a wide mix of personalities to throw together.

There is no doubt in my mind that Bellamy is the vixen. Her stunning looks and somewhat cunning personality make her the perfect candidate for the job. Although I'm surprised to learn that she is a veterinarian, the way she openly flirts with the captain and the snide comments she occasionally shoots my way make me confident that she has been cast as the fiery seductress.

Her husband, Josh, is clearly Mr. All-America. I'm not at all surprised to find out that he was a basketball star in high school. He couldn't be more of an opposite from the siren that is now his wife.

All evening, I had been considering the idea that Tiffany might have been cast as the bubble-headed blonde. While I hate to stereotype anyone, she has already made several comments that make her seem like the epitome of an airhead.

When one of our waiters tells the old joke, "Did you hear

the one about the guy who told his server that his soup tasted funny?" He waits for us to shake our heads before dropping the punch line, "The server asked him why he wasn't laughing then."

Groans and light chuckles emit from around the table. Tiffany, however, bursts out with her high-pitched, gregarious laugh. Once that dies down, she says, "I don't get it," which makes us all erupt with real laughter. I feel bad for laughing at her expense, but the blank stare she gives us before joining in with a chuckle of her own tells me we haven't hurt her feelings.

The only one who rolls his eyes at Tiffany is her newlywed husband, Paul. If anyone in the group is somewhat bookish and nerdy, it's Paul. He is shorter than the other two grooms and has wire rimmed glasses. The look works on him and he's certainly not unattractive, but I do wonder what the producers were thinking when they placed the somewhat snooty, brainiac with the ditz of the group. *Maybe they are hoping opposites attract?* I'm afraid their gamble might not pay off because Tiffany and Paul seem so far to be the least compatible of the three couples.

Looking at Cam, I'm fairly certain that he is the Prince Charming of the group. He's incredibly handsome and has already proven himself to be caring, loyal, and fun. I definitely scored the best groom. I'm confident that we can conquer the horrid kissing problem, and once we do, the sparks will probably fly.

Since they chose opposites for the other two couples, it seems odd that they chose me to marry Mr. Perfect. *Does that mean they think I am the Evil Queen?* I smile at my wayward thought. Deciding that is silly, I wonder if I really am destined to become the internet's Sweetheart. Maybe they picked the two of us because we really are well-suited for each other. It seems like an unfair advantage towards winning the money over the other two couples, but I'm not complaining.

I catch my new hubby's eye and give him a broad grin. *We've got this*, I think to myself as he rewards me with a return grin that just about knocks my socks off.

## 12

*A*ll too soon, dinner is over and it is time to return to our rooms. Not wanting to leave Cam just yet, I ask him if he'd like to go for a stroll on the upper decks. He quickly agrees and loops his arm through mine. The gesture is old-fashioned, sweet, and comfortable. It makes me feel safe and cared for, like we are a courting couple from the early 1900's, not a reality television duo that got married without ever having laid eyes on each other.

The cool breeze off the inky black water is more prevalent at night. I scoot closer to Cam seeking his warmth. He gallantly offers me his dinner jacket, and I gladly accept. The almost-full moon is shining brightly and reflecting on the flat calm ocean.

The entire romantic scenario would be almost perfect, were it not for the cameraman recording our every move. It is obvious that he is trying to be unobtrusive, but he is impossible not to notice. T.J. has warned us not to look at him or acknowledge the camera in any way, but that is easier said than done.

We walk along the railings of the top deck towards the

bow of the ship. Other passengers move past, but pay little notice to us. They have evidently been warned not to engage the 'stars' in conversation or disrupt filming in any way.

Pausing to gaze out at the seemingly endless expanse of water, Cam pulls me into his arms. When he tilts his head and moves in for a kiss, I comply, but keep my lips tightly shut. I don't want a replay of his post-wedding aggressive tongue maneuvers. I'll need to address that with him when the cameras are off.

"Shall we head down to our room?" he asks me, sounding incredibly debonair.

"OUR room?!?" I screech, forgetting for a moment about the camera.

T.J. quickly appears, as if out of thin air. He has evidently been watching the entire exchange from some hidden viewing station with a live feed of my wedding night. I try not to be irked––after all, I have agreed to let the entire world watch this play out. "Darling, darling," he gives me a condescending smile, "You just married the man. Surely, you didn't think you would maintain separate cabins?"

I don't respond because that is exactly what I thought. I'd had no reason to believe that I wouldn't be spending the duration of the cruise in my tiny cabin adjacent to Syd's transformation station. Instead, I lift my chin, feeling defiant and intending to hold my ground on this. I don't want to be portrayed as a prude on the show, but sharing a room with someone I just met––husband or not––is crossing the line.

*The other brides must also be balking at sharing rooms with their newlywed husbands, right?* I'm assuming they weren't aware of the planned sleeping arrangements either, although Cam seems to be in-the-know. This makes me wonder what else he knows that I don't. *Is he privy to some inside information? Or was this all contained in the lengthy contract that I'm now wishing I had at least perused before signing?*

Stamping my foot in frustration, I announce, "I'm not sleeping with a man I just met." The idea is preposterous, and I am frustrated that we are even having this discussion.

Cam remains quiet, apparently opting to let the smooth-talking producer handle me. "Ruthie, Babe, we have to give the viewing audience what they want, and they will want to see the happy newlyweds slip into their suite to spend their first night of unbridled passion in each other's arms. What happens inside the suite is your business. You are free to sleep on the balcony for all I care, but we need a shot of the two of you heading into the room to make your union official by consummating this marriage." My head whips around to him at the last part. "Or at least we need to make the viewers think that," he quickly amends. "Come on," he coaxes me, sliding an arm around me and starting to walk, "you won't believe the accommodations we have for you. It's a major upgrade from that closet-sized room we had you in earlier."

Not wanting to have a full-on hissy fit on camera, I acquiesce. Sharing a room with Cam is not ideal, but I guess it will give us a chance to get to know each other. He is my spouse, after all, so it probably makes sense for us to spend some time together. Shaking my head at the foreign, yet thrilling, idea of having a husband, I silently marvel at how much has already happened today.

Deciding to gracefully accept this new arrangement, I add some pep to my step as we walk to our new quarters. Vowing to use this time to get to know my new husband and to try to make the best of this sticky situation, I turn to flash a reassuring smile at Cam. He clears his throat when we reach the closed door that T.J. indicates is ours, and I realize that this is probably just as awkward for him as it is for me.

In an effort to calm us both and to make us feel more like a team, I grasp Cam's hand in mine before asking, "Shall we?"

"That's more like it," T.J. nods his approval.

Cam sweeps the door open and lets me walk in first, still firmly grasping my hand. "Wow!" I gush when I get a good look at our suite. The elegant room is large and ornate—a night and day difference from the tiny and sparse room I had used earlier.

"Let's try that one more time," T.J. suggests firmly. "This time carry her over the threshold."

"Oh, right," Cam agrees as we head back out to the hallway.

Swooping me up into his strong arms, Cam then struggles to reopen the door. T.J. leans around to twist the handle and shoves the door open for him.

Once inside, we both turn to T.J. to make sure he is happy with this entrance. He circles his hand in the air at me as if he is expecting more. When it dawns on me what he is after, I say, "Wow," but my false attempt at enthusiasm falls desperately short.

T.J. pinches the bridge of his nose with his thumb and index finger. "That will have to do," he decides, not even attempting to hide his disappointment in my unimpressive acting skills. Shuffling the cameraman out, he calls over his shoulder, "Have fun, kids!"

"We will!" Cam responds far too enthusiastically as he gently places me back on my feet. His affirmation makes me rather concerned about what he thinks is about to happen.

Relieved to be camera-free for a bit, I poke around the elegant room. Opening a drawer, I am pleased to see that my belongings have been transferred to this room and neatly put away. Opening the massive closet, I chuckle at their lack of subtlety when I see the white lacy negligee that is hanging front and center. "Yeah, right," I mutter quietly before quickly closing the door. I don't want Cam to see the skimpy ensemble and get any ideas. Grabbing some of my own sleepwear from the drawer, I escape to the bathroom.

When I emerge from the bathroom, my face has been scrubbed clean and I have donned a faded red Coca-Cola tee shirt and white cutoff sweatpants. My go-to jammies make me feel comfortable and relaxed. I am planning to try to get Cam to make his bed on the foldout sofa, but if he refuses, I will sleep there.

"Sexy," Cam remarks, not bothering to mask his sarcasm.

"I was going for comfy, not sexy," I tell him honestly, noting that he has stripped down to black boxer briefs that are undeniably bulging in all the right places. While I don't mind seeing his toned body, especially his tight rear end that I am now getting a nice view of, I'm somewhat uncomfortable that he is wearing so little clothing. We are practically strangers, after all. Reminding myself that his current outerwear is no more revealing than most swim trunks, I bend over to retrieve my fuzzy socks from the drawer.

He has the audacity to whistle at me while my booty is in the air. The high-pitched sound annoys me. It's not like I'm a piece of meat. I straighten, planning to give him a piece of my mind about respect and common decency, but when I turn, what I find leaves me utterly speechless.

Cam has shucked his underwear and is now sprawled out across the enormous California King-sized bed, like a starfish, with his limbs outstretched towards each corner of the bed. My mouth falls open and my eyes widen at the shocking sight of him––all of him. His massive erection is straining upward toward the ceiling. He brings one hand down to circle himself and rubs up and down his length a few times before saying in a husky voice, "Come and get me, Mama."

I stand there for a moment, stunned into immobility, unable to form a cohesive thought. "OMG!" I shriek, finally regaining my senses enough to cover my eyes with one hand in a feeble attempt to unsee what I had just witnessed.

"What?" His clueless question surprises me enough that I peek out between my fingers just in time to see him lean up on one elbow, his other hand still enthusiastically stroking his penis.

*Can he possibly be this clueless?* I wonder. He notices me peeking at him and flicks his tongue out at me in a disgusting come-hither gesture. *Yes, apparently he is that clueless,* I decide as I whirl around to return to the bathroom. Once inside, I click the lock into place and slide down the door to sit on the cool tile floor.

It takes him a while to respond to my exit, which makes me wonder if he gave up on having me join in on his party and decided instead to finish what he started as a solo mission. Eventually, he tentatively knocks on the door.

"What?" I ask flatly, making sure there is no friendliness that could possibly be misconstrued in my voice.

"What's wrong?" he asks, truly seeming perplexed.

For some reason, his completely insensitive and oblivious question infuriates me. "YOU are what is wrong." I yell back at him. "How could you do that?" I ask incredulously. "What were you thinking?" The questions are spilling out of me rapid-fire. I don't give him a chance to respond. "On what planet did you think that would be okay? Are you crazy??"

Realizing that I don't even want to hear his answers, I stop asking the questions that are floating through my head. He uses the silence to respond. "I don't know...am I crazy for thinking that my WIFE might want to make love on our wedding night?"

"I don't even know you," I remind him.

"But you married me," he points out. "It's implied that a couple will have sex on their wedding night. Everyone knows that."

I can't fight with his logic. The two of us just made vastly different assumptions about what would be acceptable behavior on our first night as a married couple, which also happens to be the first night we've known each other.

"It's not happening," I tell him firmly.

"Yeah, I kind of figured that out," he admits, and I decide that maybe he's not quite as dense as I had feared. "You can come out. I won't bother you any more tonight," he promises.

I don't like the fact that he added the 'tonight' on the end, and as sincere as he sounded, I visualize opening the door, only to find him standing there with his dick out and at the ready. "I think I'll sleep in here," I decide.

"Suit yourself." I hear him pad back over to the bed and shut off the lamp.

*Turns out Prince Charming isn't so charming after all,* I mumble to myself as I retrieve towels to devise a makeshift pillow and blanket before climbing into the bathtub to attempt to get some sleep.

13

"I want my old room back." I announce to T.J., who seems completely surprised to see me.

"I figured you'd be getting some rest after a raucous night of headboard banging," the producer says crassly before sliding the last bite-and-a-half of his raspberry danish into his mouth. Jamie snorts with laughter at his crude comment, solidifying my suspicion that she has a crush on him.

I had gotten up early and snuck around to avoid waking Cam. He had been sprawled across the bed and snoring loudly. He was at least wearing his black boxer briefs, which was an immense relief.

After quietly donning a hot pink bikini and a brightly-colored cover-up and exiting the room, I made a beeline for the main dining hall–– assuming I would find someone from the show eating breakfast. Tracking down T.J. was ideal because he will be able to do something about the unfortu-nate room situation. While I don't relish returning to the tiny room I started out in, I'll do that if it's the only option to get away from Cam.

"Your wedding night didn't make all of your dreams come

true?" T.J. is still being inappropriate, so I don't bother to answer. Instead, I give him a narrow-eyed glare that says I'm not backing down. Somewhat to my surprise, it works. "Okay, okay." He holds up his hands in mock surrender. "You can go back to the tiny room you used yesterday, if it's that important to you."

I smile, proud of myself for negotiating my way back to my former room, until T.J. looks at Jamie and sneers, "That hunk must be downright awful in the sack for her to be this desperate to get away from him AND the massive honeymoon suite I secured for them." Turning to me he asks, "Did you see that balcony? It's to die for."

Thoroughly annoyed by the assumptions he is making, as well as the way he is badmouthing Cam, I start to retort, but then I think better of it. Opting instead to make a break for it while I'm still ahead, I turn on my heel and flounce away with my head held high.

The fact that my hackles were raised by his criticism of my new husband cracks me up. Cam behaved like an unbelievable pig last night, and I want nothing more to do with his overt and unwanted sexual advances; nonetheless, I don't appreciate anyone else picking on him.

It's like he's already family, I decide, chuckling to myself. I'm exactly the same way with my sister. As teenagers, she and I used to get into some raging fights where I would call her names that I regretted soon after. If anyone else ever dared to say similar things about her, I would have released my inner ninja on them, and I know Roxy has always felt exactly the same way about me. We have each other's backs--as a family should.

Deciding that I'll retrieve my personal belongings after Cam is up and out of the suite (and secretly hoping that the mysterious elves that magically move and unpack my stuff will take care of that chore), I head up to the pool deck.

ANN OMASTA

Looking around, I marvel at row after row of perfectly aligned, white lounge chairs and wonder where they were stowed during our wedding ceremony. I'm pleased to find a full breakfast buffet with heaps of sizzling, delicious-smelling food. After loading my plate, I hear Syd yelling and waving me over to his table, "Ruthie...over here!"

Giving Syd and his table companions a friendly smile, I join them. After introducing me to the other stylists, Syd asks me, "Bacon much?" He grins to let me know he's teasing, as he indicates my plate that is piled high with a crispy, savory mound of bacon.

"Yesterday was rather stressful, so I feel like I deserve it," I answer simply, shrugging my shoulders.

"You go, Girl!" Syd high-fives me, but the blank stares from the other stylists indicate that they aren't impressed with me––at all.

Wondering if they are loyal to their own contestants, I choose not to take their snubbing personally. *Maybe they get a bonus if the person they assist wins,* I decide.

"My dear," Syd says seriously as he lifts a lock of the frizz on top of my head. "What has happened to your hair?"

"I slept in a bathtub and didn't take the time to tame it before bolting out of the room this morning," I deadpan.

The group at the table laughs as if they think I'm joking. "That looks more like screwed-my-brains-out-last-night hair," one of the other stylists inserts dryly.

Rather than correcting her, I shrug my shoulders. Obviously, everyone is going to think along those lines. Wanting to move the subject away from my wedding night activities, I turn to Syd. "You know what I really need?"

He shakes his head, waiting for my answer. "Sea salt spray!" I reveal.

"Well, we have plenty of that." Syd chuckles as he waves a hand out to indicate the vast ocean surrounding us.

"No, for my hair, Silly. Sea salt spray is the only thing that gives my hair texture and tames the frizzies. It's really a miracle worker. We should try to track some down."

"I'll see what I can do," Syd promises before changing the subject. "I, for one, slept like a baby last night. The gentle motion of the ship lulled me into the most restful slumber. It felt like being rocked in a cradle."

"You remember how that felt?" I ask him, surprised.

"Mm-hmm," he reveals. "My momma rocked me to sleep just last week." Lightly shoving a hand at my shoulder, Syd starts cackling at his own silly joke. The boisterous sound of his laughter is contagious and soon everyone at the table is giggling with him.

Abruptly stopping, he turns to me and asks excitedly, "Have you heard what is on the agenda for tonight?"

Having used the pause as an excuse to stuff an entire piece of bacon in my mouth, I respond with a shake of my head. I'm feeling nervous about what is coming, but I try not to let it show on my face.

"We all get to gather in the theater to watch the first show!" he exclaims, grabbing my arm like this is the most exciting news in the world.

"Already?" I ask, stunned.

"Yep--the magic of the internet, Baby. The show will stream worldwide at the click of a button," he confirms. "They are editing the video from the wedding now. By tomorrow morning, you will be a household name!"

"Yay," I say, with a lot less eagerness than Syd has shown. I was hoping for more of a chance to prove myself as a lovable person before they drop the first episode.

"It will be fab!" Syd promises.

I pray that he's right.

## 14

*A*fter breakfast, Syd insists on 'fixing' me. I shower in my tiny cabin, which (amazingly) already has my stuff in it, before letting him have his way with my hair and makeup––fully trusting him now.

When he spins me around to reveal my much less glamorous daytime look, I am pleased with the results. He has done just enough to accentuate my eyes and cheekbones, but I don't look too made-up. Turning from side to side, I admire the simple, smooth ponytail he has pulled my hair into.

"You're really talented at your job," I gush to him. "I look fantastic in about half the time it would take me to look pretty good if I were doing it myself."

"Why, thank you." He mock bows at me before leaning down to kiss my cheek and adding, "It helps when you get to start with a lovely blank canvas."

Touched by his sweet compliment, I feel my cheeks turn pink under the blush he has just expertly applied. I'm not sure if a camera is rolling in this room, but I hope they caught this tender and sincere moment for the show.

I spend the rest of the day feeling queasy with anxiety

about how I will be portrayed on the first episode of the show. Will I become beloved by the viewing audience? Or will I be shown as an awkward, accident-prone dork? They want viewers to like me, right? Maybe they will leave my mishaps on the cutting room floor.

It is apparently a somewhat schedule-free day, so I utilize the time to check out our spectacular floating home. An ever-present camera stalks behind me, recording my every move, but within a few hours, I barely notice its presence.

At one point, I see Cam walking towards me from a distance on the promenade deck. Not wanting to have an uncomfortable confrontation with him that will play out on camera, I quickly turn right to slip into a lounge and out the other side to avoid running into him.

Feeling somewhat at a loss for what to do, I decide to go up to the sun deck for a quick round of putt-putt. Tiffany and Paul are there choosing golf clubs, so I ask if I can join them. They politely agree and the three of us (and two cameramen) set off on a round of miniature golf.

Watching the two of them, I am surprised by the level of intimacy the two opposites already seem to share. Tiffany claims to have never played golf before, so Paul stands close behind her at the first hole to help her swing her club. He whispers something near her ear that makes her giggle with pleasure as she leans back into him.

I note that he gently places his hand at the small of her back as we walk to each hole and wonder if they have made a true love connection, or if this is all show for the cameras. Not wanting to be overly cynical, I decide to give them the benefit of the doubt.

Tiffany asks me where Cam is, so I tell her he went for a swim--even though I have no idea what he is actually doing, nor do I really care. For some reason, I feel almost guilty that my relationship with Cam isn't working out.

Once we finish the 9-hole course, I pretend like I have somewhere to be and wave as I shuffle away, indicating that I will see them later. They feign disappointment at my departure, but I sense they are relieved to be alone (except for their cameraman) once more.

Deciding to catch some rays and absorb a little Vitamin D, I head to the lido deck. On my way, I pass an outdoor bar where Cam and Bellamy are sharing tall, brightly hued drinks. As they clink their glasses together, I notice that she has her hand on his thigh. For some reason, this really irks me. He is my husband, after all. I don't want him, but it seems like he would refrain from hitting on other women until we can get this sham of a marriage annulled. It would be the respectful thing to do--especially since there is a camera behind them, recording the entire illicit exchange.

Not wanting to cause a scene, I put my head down and scurry quickly past. I know the camera following me has picked up on the situation, so I'm fairly certain this will be part of the drama for the second episode of the show. I just hope that I will have already won the show's audience over by then.

I briefly wonder where Josh is and what he thinks about my husband and his wife cozying up together for a drink, but I decide not to seek him out. A swapping spouses situation would probably mean ratings gold for the show, but I don't want to be portrayed as a hussy, and I'm fairly certain they are planning to insinuate that my marriage was consummated last night.

Taking the high road, I find a lounge chair with a nice view of the pool and the vast sea beyond. Before I can even get my pool towels situated to my liking, a waiter with a hot pink flowery shirt appears to see if I need anything. I squint up at him. Raising a hand to shade my eyes, I say, "Guess I should have grabbed my sunglasses."

At his grin, I continue, "It's noon somewhere, right?" He gives me a blank look and seems uncertain how to respond, so I add. "I'd love a huge, fruity, frozen concoction with lots of rum and one of those tiny umbrellas on top."

He clearly understands this because he nods, beams a huge smile at me, and hurries off to make it so. I'm barely settled before he returns and presents his tray to me. I'm delighted to find a pair of black, oversized sunglasses next to my drink.

"Wow, what service!" I gush as I grab the shades and attempt to pull off the souvenir shop's price tag. He sees me struggling and quickly comes to my aid by retrieving a small knife from his pocket and snipping off the tag.

I don the bejeweled glasses, which are a little gaudy for my taste--although I would never tell the well-meaning waiter that. He smiles and tells me I look like a movie star before moving a small table to the side of my chair and placing my drink on it.

"Mission accomplished then," I respond to his compliment before a sinking feeling begins to dawn on me. I don't have my purse or any money with me. "I need to pay you," I mutter aloud as I'm realizing the store clerk probably expects him to return payment or a signed receipt for the sunglasses.

Shaking his head, the waiter says simply, "Show pays."

"Nice!" I nod my head before adding, "In that case, pick up a pair for yourself, too."

He grins at me before scurrying away to take care of another passenger. Smiling to myself, I lean back and begin sipping the delicious alcoholic beverage he has delivered. I shiver as the coolness of the icy drink travels throughout my body. Slurping it down as quickly as I can without getting brain freeze, I set the empty glass aside and lean back in my chair.

The warmth of the sun feels glorious on my skin. I am

tempted to flag down the waiter again to ask for sunscreen so I can stay out longer, but I don't want to be viewed as a diva. I briefly consider going to the shop to purchase the lotion myself, but I don't know if the store clerk will realize who I am or will expect me to pay for the purchase. Deciding to only stay out in the sun until I begin to feel my overly-pale skin burning, I turn my head to the side to avoid mussing my ponytail and lean back onto my towel pillow.

*A*wakening with a start, I quickly realize that the sun is much further down in the sky than when I arrived at the pool. One glance at my skin indicates that I am sunburnt--really sunburnt.

I glare up at the cameraman who is filming me from the shade of a large umbrella. "Why didn't you wake me?" I demand, completely ignoring the strict instructions not to ever interact with the cameras or crew.

He shrugs his shoulders as if to say he had no choice in the matter. He looks bored, which makes me wonder if he filmed the entire time I was asleep. I wonder if I drooled or snored or did anything else embarrassing. The lounge chair had been exceedingly more comfortable than the bathtub that was my bed last night, so I slept rather soundly--hopefully not too soundly.

I glare at him as I delicately get up to return to my room. The soreness is already setting in and I fear that I will look like a lobster by dinner-time.

## 15

*A*fter taking a cool shower and gingerly donning my robe, I poke my head through the opening in the adjoining door and am pleased to find Syd waiting for me. One glimpse of my charbroiled skin makes him nearly fall out of his chair.

"Ouch, Girl! What happened to you?" he asks, although it's obvious what has happened. Without waiting for an answer, he starts digging through one of his deep makeup cases. Finding what he is after, he hands me a bright blue bottle of aloe and Lidocaine gel. "Coat yourself in this," he instructs me, "then we'll see what we can do about those raccoon eyes."

Feeling like a total doofus for allowing myself to get so burnt, I quietly return to my room to comply with his request. I'm pleasantly surprised when the cool gel provides some calming relief to my inflamed skin.

Hoping that he's not too disappointed in my lack of judgment, I sheepishly return to Syd. "Okay, Babydoll," he says kindly. "I found this loose, silky sundress that won't require you to put a bra on those raw shoulders. How does this look for dinner tonight."

I'm incredibly touched by his thoughtfulness. I try to give him a hug, but when he gently returns it his thighs brush against mine. I screech, "Ack! That hurts!"

"Sorry, Sweetness," he tells me, and I can tell he is sincere. Turning all-business, he says, "Okay, let's see what we can do about this face."

He uses a gentle touch as he works to tone down the redness on my face. The giant white circles around my eyes caused by the shade my sunglasses provided make for a bit of a challenge. Even though he grumbles about it, when he turns me towards my reflection, I'm amazed at the results. He has calmed the redness, evened out my skin tone, and lightly brushed powder down my neck and décolletage to help blend the vastly different colors of my skin so the areas beyond my ears that had been in the shade no longer looked like they have been dipped in flour.

Shuffling me next door with the sundress, he instructs me to step into it, so I don't mess up his masterpiece. Glancing into the full-length mirror after donning it, I am horror-struck to see my reflection. Having heard my gasp, Syd rushes over to see what the problem is.

One glance at me has him erupting into giggles. "It's not funny," I tell him, trying to sound stern––even though I'm beginning to join him in the hilarity. My face and neck are a dark, reddish tone, the fronts of my arms and legs are deep red, while the back-side of me looks completely white, by comparison. I look utterly ridiculous.

"What am I going to do?" I wail, once our laughter subsides.

"Don't worry. I'll take care of you." Syd reassures me, and I instantly feel better. His fix involves having me hold my sundress out of the way while he uses spray tan to even out the remarkable variation in the tone of my skin. "Does that sting?" he asks kindly as he lightly pats the dividing line to blend the colors together.

I shake my head, just wanting to get this over with. The end result of his ministrations surprises me. He has effectively blended the two vastly different colors of my skin into one dark, lovely shade. "You are a miracle worker!" I gush. "No hugs, though," I add, in order to be clear. Although the awful, two-toned color of my skin has been alleviated, the stinging tenderness has not.

Full of surprises, Syd presents me with a bottle of Bumble and Bumble Surf Spray––the brand I prefer. "How did you..." I'm unable to complete the question because I'm so stunned that he was able to secure this so quickly when we have been at sea all day.

"Anything for you, my darling." He waves off getting the sea salt spray as if it is no big deal. After generously dousing my locks with it and scrunching some loose waves into place, Syd declares me finished and sends me off to dinner.

I marvel at the man and his talents as I head down to the elegant dining room. My hopes that I won't be the last one to arrive are quickly dashed when I see everyone sitting at the Captain's table waiting for me––again.

It does not escape my notice that the seating arrangements have been modified tonight. The married couples are each still seated together. Tonight, though, Cam and Bellamy are side by side, as well. I wonder if Josh and the others have noticed how snuggly the two of them seem to be. If not, it will all be revealed on the show. This should be interesting.

Dinner is rather uneventful. The table is surprisingly quiet––probably because we are all nervous about our impending television debuts. The fancy cuisine we are presented with looks delicious, but I barely taste it as I go through the motions of eating because my stomach is so jittery.

Before I know it, the dessert plates are swept away and the Captain announces that it's time to go down to the theatre. Taking a deep calming breath, I get up to follow the others downstairs. It's a thrilling feeling to know that anyone with an internet connection can watch my wedding day unfold. I mentally cross my fingers that I'll be presented in the best possible light.

he ship's theatre is massive and crowded. The front row has been roped off for us. The special treatment makes me feel like a star already. When the lady seated behind me leans forward to pat my shoulder and wish me luck, I attempt to hide my wince of pain with a smile and politely thank her.

As the cinema's lights dim, and the dark red, velvet curtain is swept back, the anticipation in the room is palpable. I can barely contain my excitement, and I'm sure the other contestants must feel the same way.

I am seated next to Cam, and I try not to be annoyed that he and Bellamy have finagled the arrangement so they are side-by-side again. Once the opening music for the show begins, all thoughts of Cam's betrayal are swept away. My entire focus is on the enormous screen in front of us.

The show starts with introductions of our group. A beaming shot of each of us in casual wear is flashed on the screen with our first name in a fancy scrawl across the bottom. I recognize the outfit I wore during the day yesterday and realize they must have taken a shot of me right when I came aboard the ship. I appear to be in awe of my surroundings, but at least my eyes are open and I'm smiling.

After the pictures are done, Tiffany appears on the screen, and I lean around Paul to smile at her. She looks as excited as I feel––like I might burst at any moment. The first words out of her mouth on the screen are "Wow, the ocean is sooo big." This statement is followed by a few seconds of her vacantly staring out to sea. I cringe inwardly as I watch the rest of the segment, which includes short snippets of interviews with her friends and family. I hadn't realized they would be talking to people from our hometowns. It quickly becomes obvious that Tiffany has been cast as the show's airhead. Once the clip is finished, I chance a look in her direction. Surprisingly, she's still smiling. Maybe she doesn't mind being portrayed as a ditz.

Next on the screen is Tiffany's spouse, Paul. As expected, he takes every opportunity during his clip to show off how smart he is by mentioning random statistics, books he has read, and his opinion on everything from politics to organic food. He comes off as being incredibly stuffy and hoity-toity, and the few of his friends that are interviewed do nothing to sway that opinion.

I suppose the producers wanted to show how opposite Tiffany and Paul are, but they ended up not showing either of them in a favorable light. They are both smiling at the screen and holding hands, so I guess maybe they are pleased with the show's outcome.

The show breaks for a word from its sponsors, and I try to breathe deeply. I've become so nervous that I've been unknowingly holding my breath. The butterflies I had in my stomach before the wedding feel like they have turned into bats, fluttering their wings and trying to escape. I refuse to vomit, despite the cold sweat I have broken into.

Cam turns my way briefly and notes the chill bumps that

have arisen on my bare arms. He gallantly offers me his dinner jacket, which I politely decline. I am certain the rough fabric would feel like sandpaper on my sunburnt skin. Cam shrugs his shoulders and raises his brows as if to say, "I tried," before turning his attention back to Bellamy.

The show resumes with Bellamy on the giant screen. Her long, red hair absolutely pops on camera, making her look stunning. I turn to catch her beaming at her likeness on the screen. Bellamy's friends and family talk about her mesmerizing beauty and how everyone in school wanted to be like her. It doesn't take long to confirm that she has been cast as the show's beautiful siren. The role suits her to a tee.

When her part ends, Cam leans over to whisper something in her ear, which makes her preen. I watch her hand slide up his thigh, and I try not to get riled up. I wish they weren't being quite so obvious about their lust for each other. Cam was selected as my husband, not hers. Realizing that I have no right to be upset since I don't want Cam for myself, I decide, again, to take the high road and ignore their public displays of affection.

The screen captures my attention once more as Josh appears. His blond hair and blue eyes translate well to the giant motion picture. He looks like the consummate Mr. All-American-Apple-Pie-Sweet-Boy-Next-Door and his self-effacing, Southern charm only adds to the persona. His mother, basketball coach, and a former girlfriend all attest to his perfection before the show goes to another commercial break.

My legs are bouncing nervously in the seat. Cam and I must be next. *Are they saving the best for last? What role will I portray in the show? Will I become America's Sweetheart? Am I going to be an internet sensation? I hope I'm not shown as the klutz who doesn't fit in.* When the insecurities start to creep in, I do my best to shut them down and think positively.

I don't have too long to worry because the show starts back up. Breaking the format, they start with Cam this time, rather than the female as they had with the other couples. The blood is pounding in my ears, but I try to focus on watching Cam's debut. He looks rakishly handsome, as I'd known he would. He has clearly been cast as the magnetic ladies' man, and he fits the bill. A string of beautiful ladies from Cam's past all rave about his devilishly-handsome looks, impeccable style, and undeniable charisma.

I wonder why Cam and Bellamy weren't put together as a couple. *Did the producers intend for them to fall for each other, despite having other spouses? Is that part of the drama of the show?*

I'm about ready to bounce out of my chair as Cam's piece finishes. Since he has been portrayed as the stud muffin, perhaps I am the sexy seductress. Shaking my head, I decide Bellamy is already clearly filling the role of temptress.

I don't have to remain curious about my role for too long. The first words out of my mouth when my turn finally comes and I appear on screen are, "Don't you know who I am?" I had said that when I had been trying to gain access to the ship without a ticket, but the way the film has been cut, it looks like I expected and demanded the star treatment.

I watch in horror as a montage of creatively-edited videos of me appear on the screen. "A random, handsome stranger bringing me to new heights of ecstasy on a casting couch...my dreams of fame are already coming true. I will make it. You'll see...America will love me. The world will love me."

I hadn't realized hidden cameras were filming any of that. Plus, they took my words completely out of context. The 'casting couch' comment had been after Syd had rubbed my back. It hadn't meant anything at all like the show insinuated. "Oh no," I drop my head and put a hand over my eyes, but the clips keep on playing.

Cringing at the way my recorded voice sounds, I hear it say to Syd, "What if I can't stand the guy they've chosen for me?" Continuing on as if Syd hasn't responded--even though he did in real life--my likeness says, "I get a tropical vacation, I have a good chance of becoming famous, I might win loads of cash, and worst case scenario is that it ends up not being a good match, and I get a divorce."

I sound like a horrid, spoiled-rotten brat. It would appear that I have been cast as the show's biotch, I realize, my heart sinking. *America isn't going to love me...they are going to hate me.*

Dropping my hands from my face, I decide I might as well watch my televised demise--everyone else I know probably is. I look up at the screen just in time to see myself preening in front of Syd's full-length mirror in my wedding dress. "Wow, I'm a beautiful bride!"

The video cuts to my sister, Roxy. I am surprised and pleased to see her. Since she lives in Hawaii now, I don't get to hang out with her nearly as much as I would like. Seeing her brings me a great deal of relief. She loves me and will straighten out this mess. "I'm lucky to be Ruthie's older sister." She smiles at the camera and a tiny bit of hope begins to take root inside me, until she continues. "No one knows her better than I do. She has always LOVED being the center of attention, so this show is perfect for her." She is grinning, and I'm sure there hadn't been any malice intended by her words, but she managed to make me look even worse.

Macy appears, smiling on the giant screen with the words 'Ruthie's BFF' under her likeness. I'm appalled to hear her say, "Ruthie's a little flighty, sometimes selfish, and a bit of a hot mess--but we love her anyway."

By the time my beloved, crazy grandma, Baggy pops up on the screen, I have already figured out how this ridiculous fiasco is going to go--they are portraying me as being completely spoiled and unlikable. In typical Baggy fashion, she says, "Ruthie has always been like a just-castrated bull on a sugar-high in a china shop, just like her Bad Grandma." Baggy indicates herself with her thumb before waggling her eyebrows and preening on the screen. "What are you doing later?" she has turned her watery gaze beyond the camera as she speaks directly to the cameraman before blowing him a kiss.

The clip ends with me saying, "You know what I really need?...Sea salt spray!" A graphic with the words "You're in the middle of the ocean!" appears on the screen just before a helicopter is shown landing on the top deck of the ship and a man retrieves a brown box labeled *Bumble and Bumble Surf Spray*. That had all just happened today. I am shocked that they were able to include the clip so quickly. That is part of the beauty of internet television, I guess. Apparently, they are able to work technological miracles if it means making me look more spoiled and selfish. Syd's voice sounds on the screen saying, "Anything for you, my darling," as a still shot of me giving a snide smile is displayed for the entire world to see.

Finally, the show breaks for some commercials. I bow my head, wishing I could turn back time to make this all go away––despite knowing that the footage will survive on the internet for eternity. Even I can't stand this version of myself. *How could anyone else like me?* My throat is burning with unshed tears. When I finally look up, Bellamy actually gives me a slightly pitying look, which lets me know without a doubt that I must now be the most hated woman in America––and likely the whole planet, thanks to the World Wide Web.

I feel frozen in my seat, unsure how to react. I want to get up and give the producers a piece of my mind for portraying me in such an awful light, but that would only serve to give them additional fodder for use on the show.

The show returns and continues along the same vein from before. Our weddings play out on the screen. The scene is picturesque and perfect, with the exception of my interruptions, which they show——including the numerous (apparently superfluous) "Cuts!" that had been called. Somehow, they manage to make it all look like intentional stunts I pulled to gain additional attention.

The camera closes in on my face as I recoil from Cam's invasive kiss. Afterward, his likeness is beaming and gawking around, while I am clearly displeased. Real-life Cam turns from the screen to give me a dirty look before shifting in his seat towards Bellamy. He evidently hadn't been aware of my less-than-pleasant reaction to our wedding kiss.

Even the pool accident comes off on the show as if I had purposely shoved Bellamy and the Captain into the water. Bellamy glares at me——with no trace of sympathy left——as if she now believes this is how things actually went down. I knew that she suspected it might have been intentional, but now she evidently thinks she has video proof.

I want to shout at her that the video is deceiving. I want to let them all know that this isn't a fair depiction of me. But how can I? They have all seen what looks like my appalling behavior with their own eyes. Everyone I know, plus millions of other people, have likely just seen it.

The show comes to a close and the others jump up to hug and congratulate each other. I sit glued to my chair——too shell-shocked to move. As worried as I was about the show's debut, in actuality it was at least a thousand times worse than I imagined.

T.J. hops up on the stage and asks everyone to please sit down for some announcements. He is looking at his cell phone as he says, "Preliminary numbers for the show's ratings are excellent!"

The crowd claps excitedly as he continues. "There are

already some new hashtags that are trending on Twitter. Two involve the show's name," he announces, "#Cruisingfor-Love and #CruisingforLoveRocks."

Some whoops and whistles erupt in the crowd. I wish I could join in the merriment, but I feel like I have been taken advantage of. I am also cursing the speed and all-encompassing nature of the internet. If I had known I would be portrayed so horribly, I never would have agreed to do the show.

T.J. continues as if I am not having the absolute worst night of my life. "One is about the hot, new couple that the world is rooting for...#TeamCamBell."

Cam and Bellamy beam at each other before hugging over this news. Even though they hadn't been shown on the screen as a couple, the show's viewers had evidently decided that they would be perfect together. I roll my eyes, now confident that this was intended to happen all along. The cynical side of me thinks that the show's producers probably planted that particular hashtag.

"And finally," T.J. adds, pausing for dramatic suspense, making me worry about what is probably coming. "The top trending hashtag on all of Twitter at the moment," he pauses once more to build the suspense, "is #IHateRuthie!"

He makes this announcement like it is the greatest news in the world. I feel like climbing under my chair and never coming out.

*How did this happen? How did I become the villain? I was supposed to be America's Sweetheart, not the most hated woman on earth.*

I shake my head in disbelief. I just want to wake up and realize this was all some horrid nightmare. I look around as tears pool and threaten to fall--the horrid nightmare part is true, but it's happening in real-life.

T.J. has left the stage and well-wishers from the rest of

the audience are making their way forward to congratulate us. It takes me a moment to process the fact that no one is coming up to me. The other five all have people surrounding them--giving them hugs and lavishing praise on them. I, however, am standing alone. I don't blame the crowd. After all, how do you tactfully approach someone about becoming a trending internet sensation for being so hated?

I quietly slip out of the auditorium, seeking solitude.

## 17

*S*yd chases me down the hallway. "Ruthie! Wait up," he calls.

I don't want to see him or anyone else right now. My ever-present camera is here to capture the moment. Plus, I now know there are cameras hidden all over the ship, so the viewing audience won't have to miss a moment of my meltdown. The tears I had been attempting to stifle are now running freely down my cheeks. I'm fairly confident they are leaving mascara streaks to serve as further evidence that I am indeed the hot mess my BFF has told the world I am.

I'm not in any mood to talk. I just want to be alone, but Syd is not having any part of that. He easily catches up to me and gently touches my arm—evidently remembering about my sunburn. "Are you okay?" he asks me, seeming honestly concerned.

"Did you know?" I turn on him. "Did you know I would be portrayed that way?" I feel like lashing out at someone, and he is the only one around.

"No, Honey, I promise I didn't know." His words sound sincere. He reaches out to tenderly swipe the back of his finger under each of my eyes, evidently clearing the black mascara trail.

I want to believe him. It feels like he is my only friend left in the world. I know the show has creatively cut the clips from my loved ones to put me in the worst possible light, but it still hurts. I hiccup on a sob as I try to say, "Everyone hates me."

Pulling me into a gentle hug, he coos, "It's going to be okay." He holds me for a long time, while I release all of my pent up anger, frustration, and hurt feelings. An older couple decked out in fancy, black eveningwear approach us in the hallway, giving us a strange look. "Nothing to see here," Syd informs them, waving them on, so they scurry past.

Releasing me from his hug and turning to the cameraman, Syd breaks our only rule, by addressing him directly. "Could you give us a few minutes?"

The guy raises his shoulders and shakes his head as if the matter is out of his control. Digging in his pocket Syd retrieves a twenty-dollar bill from his money clip. "Please," he adds as he hands over the money.

Pocketing the cash, the cameraman turns off the record button and heads into the adjacent bar without a word. We briefly hear the haunting singing voice of a woman in a sparkling pink gown sitting atop a grand piano as he opens and closes the door of the lounge.

"Thank you," I tell Syd, and I mean it. I hadn't realized how draining it is to have the camera constantly recording my every movement—especially now that I know the footage is being used to show me in such an incredibly unfavorable light.

"There are still plenty of hidden cameras," Syd waves a hand around our surroundings, reminding me that I'm not completely off the hook.

I nod in acknowledgement of his warning as he gives me

a sad look. "I wish I could make this better for you." He sounds sincere.

"I feel like I'm all alone in the world," I reveal to him.

"I'm here, Baby," he says kindly. I nod again, trying to be brave and not wanting to point out that I've only known him for two days.

"You miss your family, though," he guesses correctly. At my nod, he goes on, "And you want to make sure that they still love you."

His assessment is spot-on, and a couple more tears escape as I nod at him. "I'm sure they do, Sweetheart," he reassures me. "They probably all said loads of wonderful things about you in front of the camera, but the show manipulated the one thing they said that could be construed as less than flattering to make it look like you are spoiled rotten."

I lean back on the railing, unconcerned about falling. I know in my heart that what Syd has said is true. My family and friends still love me, but seeing them on screen adding fuel to the 'hate Ruthie' fire had been overwhelming and sad. "I wish I could see the entire videos that were filmed with each of them," I admit to Syd.

"I'm sure they are all just as upset about the rotten portrayal as you are," he reminds me.

"You think so?" My voice sounds hopeful. It's not that I want them to feel bad, but I would like to know for sure that they hadn't intended to make me looks so horrible.

Syd nods, then his eyes widen with an idea. "Come with me." He grabs my hand, pulling me behind him.

I follow him into a tiny ladies room. He drags me inside and snicks the lock into place. "You shouldn't be in here," I remind him.

"It's okay," he reassures me before adding, "there won't be any cameras in here."

Comprehension dawns as he pulls a cell phone out of his

pocket. "One call," he tells me, before adding sternly, "And if you tell anyone, I'll deny it."

"I won't tell a soul," I promise, grabbing the phone greedily. I don't have to think long about who to call, especially since her number is one of the few that I know by heart in this day of automatic dialing.

She picks up on the first ring. Rather than a traditional greeting, she answers by saying, "I'm going to give those snot-nosed, lying, television turds a piece of my mind!"

I have no idea how she knew I was on the other end of the phone, since I'm using Syd's cell, but her fired-up, no-nonsense response immediately makes me feel better. "Baggy," I breathe a sigh of relief as I talk to my wild, crazy, grab-'em-by-the-balls-and-never-let-go grandmother.

## 18

Feeling a great deal better after my chat with Baggy, I emerge from my bathroom hideaway with Syd. Knowing now how the producers of the show want to portray me, I figure they'll try to make it look like he and I shared a forbidden rendezvous in the ladies' room. I refuse to worry about that right now, though.

Not wanting to run into anyone from the show, but too jacked up to sleep, I turn to Syd with a questioning look. Sensing my dilemma, he takes my hand. "I have an idea. Come with me."

I gladly follow him, feeling relieved to let him do all the thinking. When he pushes the elevator button for the fifth floor, I start to become slightly nervous. Thankfully, he leads me in the opposite direction of the 'theatre of shame,' where my fiasco of an internet television debut had just occurred.

When we reach the smaller theatre at the back of the ship—at least I think it's the back, although I still get turned around in the vessel's enormous interior—I balk about entering. "I don't want to be around people," I inform Syd, although I would have thought he should already know that.

"This is where the overflow crowd from the show's debut had to go," he reveals. "Our theatre was standing room only, so the people in here have no idea what happened." He points to a Broadway-style poster that indicates there is a magic-comedy act in progress.

I don't feel a bit like watching a cheesy comedian. My face must have betrayed my reluctance because Syd leans in to convince me. "It will be dark in there, and we can partake in some adult beverages."

"You had me at dark." I smile at him. A lack of light means that cameras won't be able to watch my every move. It's amazing how quickly my feelings about having my every word and gesture recorded have changed. Just yesterday, I loved the attention because it made me feel special and sought after. Now...not so much.

We try to slip quietly into the back of the theatre. I sure don't need a snarky comedian picking on me for arriving late to his show. It takes a bit for our eyes to adjust to the black room. We find an empty two-top table at the back and claim it.

Immediately, a perky waitress in a short, black skirt appears to take our drink order. Syd orders us each a mojito. That probably wouldn't have been my first choice, but as long as the beverage has alcohol in it, I'm not going to complain.

Our mojitos quickly arrive and I am pleasantly surprised to find the cool drink is tastier than I would have expected. I take a couple of healthy gulps before turning my attention to the stage. Something about the stance of the man in the spot-light catches my attention.

His dark hair, broad shoulders, and slender hips are undeniably attractive. The tight black tee shirt he is wearing makes it obvious that he is in great shape. There is something familiar about him that I can't quite pinpoint, though. I

87

watch him, mesmerized. I find myself listening to the lilt of his voice, but not really his words.

I sense the moment he sees me. His eyes lock on mine, and he smiles, making two huge, gorgeous dimples. I feel bowled over by his gaze––at least I hope he's looking at me. Now I wish we had sat closer to the stage.

Even as I'm telling myself that the stage lights must be in his eyes and that he couldn't possibly have been looking at me, Syd leans over to whisper, "Did you see the way he just looked at you? I'd give anything to have that hunk of beef-cake look at me like that!"

I smile at Syd in acknowledgment, but don't respond. My eyes quickly dart back to the man on stage. Suddenly, it hits me who he looks like. My breath turns quick and shallow. It *can't* be him. I shake my head, trying to clear my thoughts. *What are the chances?* I wonder.

Trying to convince myself that my mind is playing some kind of trick on me, I lean over to Syd. "What is the performer's name?" I ask him.

Making a quiet request of the lady sitting next to us, Syd accepts the offered paper program and hands it to me. I squint to see the words in the dim lighting. When I finally make out the name of tonight's headliner, I nearly fall out of my seat––Andrew Stark, the exact man whose picture I gaze at almost every night before bed.

## 19

*F*eeling like I might suffocate or hyperventilate, I get up and run from the darkened theatre. Before long, Syd follows me. "What's wrong, Sweets?" he asks, sounding truly concerned.

"Do they know? How can they know? Is he a plant? Is this a trick?" I ask Syd desperately. Even though deep-down I know that he has no idea what I'm talking about, I can't seem to stop asking him the questions that are burning through my brain. Syd's bewildered expression confirms that I have thoroughly confused him. "They can't know, can they?"

"Who can't know what? You're not making any sense. You're going to have to back up a little."

"The magic man in there," I point to the theatre doors, "is *the one that got away* from me." I inform Syd as I run my hands through my hair and slide down the wall to sit on the floor.

Syd only hesitates for a moment before joining me on the plush primary-colored, geometric-patterned carpet. "Tell me," he says simply.

"Andrew was my high school crush." I reveal.

When I pause, Syd inserts, "He's held up well over the years. That guy is a dreamboat."

Nodding and smiling at him, I continue. "He was always just out of reach, but not in the way you would think." At Syd's curious look, I expand. "He wasn't the stereotypical irresistible athlete, despite his hot body. He was more of an artsy, moody, musician type."

"Ahhh, one of those." Syd smiles down at me. "They're always more difficult to land than the dumb jocks."

I nod, acknowledging that Syd is right about that. "I spent all of one song in his arms, dancing on Prom night, and it was heaven."

"Spill," Syd leans in--all ears.

"He was a Senior, and I was a Junior," I start.

"I already have chill bumps," Syd squeals, showing me his arm as proof.

"It's not a great love story," I tell him before admitting, "Well, maybe a one-sided one."

"Uh oh, I don't like the sound of that, but go on." Syd urges me.

"I had an enormous crush on him, and I did everything in my power to make him notice me. I tried short skirts, blatant flirting, and even parading around on the arm of the quarter-back of the football team, but Andrew never seemed to take notice of me."

"He was playing hard to get," Syd guesses.

"Or he just wasn't interested," I say sadly.

"Not possible," Syd tells me kindly.

Smiling at him, I continue with my story. "He was always just out of reach for me, and it drove me absolutely crazy. I had never before--or ever since-- had a man turn down my advances. You being the exception to that, of course." I nudge him gently with my elbow to let him know I'm teasing.

"I'd totally go for you, if I was into ladies," he grins at me.

"Right," I say sarcastically. Not wanting him to feel required to flatter me, I shift back into my story. "Anyway, he didn't seem interested in me at all, which, of course, made me want him even more. I used to finagle my schedule so that I would pass him in the hallways at school. Everywhere I went, I took the long route so I could drive past his house and snoop to see if his light was on or if he had anyone over."

"Stalker alert," Syd teases me.

"No kidding," I admit. "But it was so much more than that to me. I wanted to be where he was, to listen to him talk or breathe, or to just watch him. It was like I came alive when I was in his presence. It was an overpowering feeling, but the more I tried to deny it, the worse it became."

"It sounds like you were obsessed with him," Syd says carefully.

"I guess I kind of was, but not in a creepy, keep-him-locked-up-in-the-basement kind of way. I wanted him to want to be with me, and it devastated me that he didn't, but I would have never forced him into anything."

"Glad to hear it," Syd gives me a reassuring smile.

I can't believe that I am sharing all of this with Syd, but it is a relief to finally be revealing the truth. My family knew that I had an enormous crush on Andrew, but I never talked about it so openly with anyone. Deciding that I've gone too far to turn back now, I forge on. "Anyway, you can imagine how thrilled I was when there was a huge upset in the voting for Senior Prom King and he beat out the superstar jock that was expected to win."

"Awesome! I love when stuff like that happens. It's just like the movies," Syd gushes.

"It felt like a movie when the head cheerleader / girlfriend to said jock ran off the stage crying and yelling about how *this wasn't how things were supposed to work out*."

"What a biotch––trying to ruin the hot band geek's big moment." Syd was clearly on the right side.

"I'm glad she did that, though," I admit, "because the principal was so befuddled by her abrupt departure that he announced that the Junior Prom Queen would be doing the spotlight dance with the Senior Prom King, rather than the runner-up Queen for the Seniors, who it probably rightfully should have been."

"Yay!" Syd actually claps with excitement over my story. "So, you and Andrew got to dance in front of everyone at his Senior Prom?"

I nod in confirmation, thrilled to see that Syd is clearly in my corner. "I was all glammed up for Prom, and he looked incredibly dashing in his black tuxedo. He pulled me into his warm embrace, and I nearly melted on the spot. He was a graceful and firm leader as he guided me around the dance floor. He smelled like fresh pine needles and chocolate." I close my eyes, still able to recall the scent having relived it so many times in my memory. Lost in the story, I continue, "I can still feel the chills that raced down my spine as our fronts lightly brushed against each other as we moved together as one. His hot breath near my ear made every inch of my body tingle with excitement. It was the most perfect few minutes of my life. If I could choose to freeze any moment in time, it would be while I was in his arms. To this day, anytime I hear the song 'In Your Eyes' by Peter Gabriel, I stop whatever I'm doing and am immediately transported back to that glorious moment in time."

"Wow." Syd says simply. He has clearly been swept into my story.

"Yeah, wow," I agree before sharing the rest of the story. "He returned to his abandoned date immediately after our life-altering-for-me dance, and the rest is history. He graduated and moved to Las Vegas to pursue his dream of becoming a famous showman. My mom occasionally runs into his mom at the grocery, so I get regular updates on his accomplishments. I try to be in all the right places the rare times he comes home to visit, but I never seem to be lucky enough to run into him."

"Well, he's here now," Syd reminds me with an excited look on his face.

"Yeah, about that," I start. "Do you think it might be too big of a coincidence that he is conveniently here while the show is filming?"

"Paranoid much?" Syd teases me.

"There's one thing I haven't told you yet," I admit. At his raised eyebrows, I add, "I have a school picture of him that I like to look at pretty much every night. I'm not still obsessed or anything," I quickly add wanting to squash any concerns he may have about my mental stability. "It's just that I like to remind myself that it's possible to feel so wonderful with another human being, and I don't want to ever settle for anything less than that kind of all-consuming passion."

"I guess that makes sense," Syd admits.

"It's really more of a reminder of how love can feel, than of Andrew himself." I'm still trying to justify keeping the picture and allowing it to be such an important keepsake so many years later. At Syd's understanding nod, I go on. "The picture is in my suitcase, and someone unpacked all of my things for me. They didn't move the picture, but do you suppose they saw it and told one of the producers?"

Syd's bright blue eyes widen in surprise at me. "So, you think someone found that tiny picture tucked away in your luggage and took it to the producers, who then researched who it could be before returning it to your bag, had someone track down the person from the picture and bring him aboard the ship to do a show in the hopes that you might stumble into each other on a cruise with thousands of passengers and rekindle your high school almost-romance?"

"Well, it sounds a little far-fetched when you put it like that." I grin at him until we both start laughing at my paranoia.

## 20

*I*t isn't long until people start filing out of the theatre. Syd and I remain in our spot on the floor watching them go. Logically, I know that I should get up and return to my room, but the chance of getting to see Andrew again––even if he just quickly passes by us––is too tempting to miss.

Seeming to understand my desire, Syd sits quietly by my side. A few of the people emerging from the theatre give us strange looks for sitting on the floor, but most pass by without giving us a second glance. Eventually, the crowd diminishes to just a trickle, but there is still no sign of Andrew.

The door hasn't opened for several minutes, and I am beginning to feel like someone standing by the microwave waiting for that last kernel of popcorn to pop as I stare at it. Just when I am beginning to wonder if he has exited the theatre via some backstage employee-only area, the door bursts open, startling Syd and me.

"Oh good, you're still here." Andrew beams a smile at me before sending a questioning gaze in Syd's direction.

I nudge Syd gently with my elbow and he quickly gets the hint. "I bet you two have some catching up to do, and I'm beat." He stretches out his arm and gives an overly dramatic fake yawn to prove his point. After getting up, he says, "Great show," to Andrew before turning to me to add, "See you in the morning." He starts walking away before turning back to look directly at me to say, "Don't do anything I wouldn't do...but that doesn't limit you very much!"

We can hear him cackling at his own joke as he saunters down the hallway. Andrew chuckles at him before plopping down on the floor right beside me. "It *is* you." His head is turned so that his ginormous sapphire eyes are gazing into mine.

My body is acutely aware of each place where our bodies are grazing each other--my shoulder, hip, thigh and the side of my foot are all zinging with electrified energy at his touch--my painful sunburn completely forgotten. Syd and I had been sitting just as close together, but it was nothing like this life-affirming feeling of being next to Andrew again. I struggle to stay completely present in the moment, savoring the feeling because I know that I will want to relive this scene with him over and over again.

It is as if no time has passed. Just seeing him has transported me back to high school and the intense feelings I have always had for him are front and center once more. Something about this man sets my body alive. I can feel my breath quickening, my pulse racing, and my nerve endings smoldering from his close proximity. I know that my body's visceral chemical reaction to him doesn't make any sense. After all, he could be a serial killer for all I know, but my physiological response to him is undeniable and uncontrollable--not that I would want to tame it, even if I could.

Even as many times as I've relived the precious few minutes I spent in his arms, my memories pale in comparison to actually being near him. The rush of his presence is an incomparable, exhilarating high that I have never experienced elsewhere. I drink it in like my parched, sunburnt skin absorbs refreshing aloe vera gel.

Realizing that my silence has dragged into the zone of what should feel awkward, I finally respond to his comment. "It's me," I affirm, smiling at him before adding, "and *you*."

"I've thought about you so many times over the years," Andrew remarks.

His revelation would have floored me had I not already been sitting on the floor. If he had any idea of the sheer number of times I have thought of him and our brief but marvelous time together, he would probably be somewhat frightened. Deciding it to be in my own best interest to play down my obsession with him, I tell him, "I have fond memories of you too."

*There, that was nice, but non-committal.* I silently commend myself for playing it somewhat cool when all I really want to do is proclaim my nonsensical intense feelings for this man, whom I barely know.

"Remember my Senior Prom night when we danced together?" he asks me, obviously having no idea how obsessed I was--*okay, am*--with him. At my nod, he continues, "What was the song they played?"

"It was 'In Your Eyes,' I think." I'm proud of myself for adding on the 'I think.' I certainly don't want to come off like a crazy person who relives that moment in time over and over every time that song comes on--even when I purposely play it on my phone.

"Yeah," Andrew nods, "I love that song."

"Me too," I confirm, deciding it's safe to admit that much to him.

"We should go down to one of the dance clubs to request they play it, so we can dance to it and relive our glory days!"

Andrew seems excited about his idea, but I'm sure he can't possibly feel one thousandth as thrilled as I do at his suggestion--especially that he referred to it as 'our glory days.' I'm sure he wasn't referring to our dance specifically with that saying, but it felt wonderful to hear him say it, nonetheless.

"Let's go!" I let some enthusiasm show in my voice, but not to the degree that I feel it.

Proving that he's still a gentleman, Andrew helps me up off the floor and hooks his elbow with mine. It is as if I am walking on air as he escorts me to one of the ship's nightclubs.

## 21

*I*t takes a bit for my eyes to adjust to the dark room. The pounding music makes the parquet dance floor seem to pulse and the swirling lights from the disco ball make the sequins on several ladies' dresses sparkle.

Under normal circumstances, the swaying motion of the ship when combined with the loud thumping of the music and the flashing lights would instigate a near-instantaneous migraine, but my body is too hyped-up over seeing Andrew to have any sort of negative reaction--even to the intense sensory overload of the discotheque.

The good news about all of the lights and noise is that filming in here would be nearly impossible. I'm not quite ready to share my lifelong crush with the world, especially knowing the producers will find some way to make it look seedy.

Andrew holds up his pointer finger at me and goes to make a request of the deejay. After much gesturing and yelling, the disc jockey nods, seeming to understand the message Andrew is trying to relay in the loud club--or perhaps the deejay is simply trying to get him to go away.

Returning, Andrew leads me onto the dance floor where we jump and raise our arms in the air for the next couple of booming fast-tracks. Neither of us are terrific dancers, but we fit right in with most of the others--who seem to have thrown their inhibitions overboard into the international waters.

After the third song ends, the deejay makes an announcement, "Time to slow it down, by special request."

'In Your Eyes' begins playing. A few disappointed twenty-somethings head to the bar for refreshment, but the vast majority of our comrades on the dance floor pair off to slow dance. Several people who had been milling around the bar or sitting at tables waiting for this moment crowd into the dancing area.

There are so many people that Andrew and I are jostled several times. Not allowing the moment to be ruined, Andrew pulls me closer to him and I lean my head on his shoulder. Immediately, I am transported in my mind back to our glorious Prom night when we previously danced together to this song.

Tonight feels the same, only better. Andrew's shoulders are broader, and he's more filled out. It is just as marvelous being engulfed in his embrace as I remembered. Some small portion of my brain feared that I built it up so much in my memory that reality would never be able to live up to my expectations. It is an immense relief to find that he is just as magnetic, charming, and sexy as I remember.

On Prom night, we had each been with other dates, but now we are adults, with nothing to stand in our way should we decide to take things farther. Well, nothing except my makeshift husband. I won't let that sham of a marriage stop me from following my destiny, though. *That has to be what this is, right? What else besides destiny would bring the man of my dreams onto the very cruise ship where I am filming a show called*

*'Cruising for Love?' Just because the producers intended for me to fall for someone else doesn't mean that I can't have found the real thing on my own.*

Andrew rubs his palm up and down on my lower back, leaving a tingling trail in the wake of his touch. I feel safe, happy, and fully alive in his arms, and I don't want the song to ever end.

All too soon, the song does end and the deejay puts on a pulsing, loud, and fast song that makes everyone jump in time to the beat. Andrew releases his hold on me, and I reluctantly let my arms drop from around his neck. There are too many people to distance our bodies from each other, which is just fine by me.

When Andrew feigns fanning himself with one hand to indicate that it is rather warm and points a thumb at the exit door, I nod and accept his outstretched hand, allowing him to lead me out of the club. "Phew," he says when we emerge. "That's the most dancing I've done since..." he seems to be thinking back, "probably Senior Prom," he decides.

I nod. It's been a while since I've been out dancing, too, but not quite that long. When he suggests we take a walk outside on the upper decks, I quickly agree. Enjoying the feeling of his hand at the small of my back, I lead the way to the stairs.

Once we have climbed our way to the top of the ship, we find a secluded spot at the railing and gaze up at the inky sky. "I've never seen so many stars," I gush and mean it. It seems like the entire atmosphere is lit up for us with glimmering twinkles. The surprisingly bright moon is shimmering on the black water.

He nods, agreeing with my assessment. "Being on a ship in the open ocean makes me feel at peace. It's a great reminder of how small we are."

"And it's nice to be so far away from the rest of the world," I insert.

"The rest of the world isn't so bad," he teases me.

"Yeah, unless you are the most hated woman in it," I say sadly.

"What? Never." He sounds genuinely taken aback.

Deciding it's time to confess what has happened, I spill the story of my ill-conceived wedding and disaster television debut that occurred over the last couple of days. *Has it only been that long? It feels like eons since we left shore.*

"You're married??" Andrew drops his arm from around my shoulders, and I miss it immediately. The bubbling chemistry that had undeniably been sizzling between us immediately dissipates on his end at my revelation.

"Yes, but it's really just a sham," I tell him desperately. "It was all for the show. I had never even seen Cam before the ceremony." The more I try to explain the situation, the worse it sounds, and I can see the distaste growing on Andrew's face.

"I should escort you back to your room," he decides abruptly.

"Okay," I agree sadly. I can feel my second chance with him slipping away, but I don't know what to do to rescue it.

All too soon, we arrive at my door and he bids me goodnight. It feels too final, like the end. I stand in my doorway and watch the only man who has ever made me feel so completely exquisite disappear down the long hallway.

## 22

*This is crazy,* I decide as I watch 'the one who got away' getting away again. Knowing that I need to do something to rescue this situation, but unsure how to go about that, I follow him--at a safe distance, of course.

We walk for what seems like an eternity before he pulls out a key card and inserts it into a door lock. He turns his head slightly to the side as he enters, and I jump back into a doorway praying that he can't see me and that whoever is in this particular room does not decide to leave and find me lurking in their narrow entry. It would probably startle us both to high heaven.

I hear Andrew's door close and decide it is safe to return to being visible in the hallway. Walking down to stand in front of his door, I contemplate my next move. I raise my hand a couple of times thinking that I'll knock, but end up lowering it because I have no idea what I can say to fix this dreadful situation.

Not knowing what else to do, I sullenly return to my own room. Walking out to my miniscule balcony, I lean out to see if I can see down to Andrew's room. Not being able to see very far, I consider standing on the tiny plastic footstool so that I can lean out farther. Deciding that would be a recipe for disaster––like falling overboard in the middle of the ocean––I opt not to risk leaning too far over the railing.

I like knowing that out of this enormous ship and the thousands of available cabins, Andrew is on the same level and side as I am. There is only an interminably long hallway and numerous tiny rooms separating us.

I wonder if he is in his bed and what he wears to bed. *Does he sleep naked? Did he immediately fall asleep when his head hit the pillow?* I'm guessing that he isn't obsessing over every word of our interaction tonight, like I am. *Is he concerned at all about the idea of not seeing me again, or has he already forgotten about it?* I fear that he has already released me from his mind. I'm also fairly certain that I will never be able to let it go.

I lie down on my bed––fully clothed––but my mind is whirling with too much activity to allow even the possibility of sleep. Sitting bolt upright, a frightening thought over-whelms me. *What if he is leaving when the ship docks tomorrow?* I had heard on the evening announcements that we would be spending the day in port at an island. I'm not sure how the entertainment gigs work. Are the entertainers on board for the duration of the cruise or do they disembark and fly home from the tiny island airport, while the next entertainer flies in to catch the ship for the next segment?

My guess is that they don't want the same people doing shows for the duration of the cruise. They probably bring in fresh talent––meaning that Andrew could be leaving. I *can't* let him go without sharing my feelings with him. I refuse to spend the rest of my life regretting not taking what might be my last chance with him. I already know that no one else has ever made me feel the way he does. There is a good chance that no one ever will have the same effect on me. I *will not* let him slip out of my grip a second time without giving it my best shot.

Feeling determined, I march down the hallway towards his room. Once there, the insecurities set in. I raise my hand to knock and lower it several times. *What if he sends me away? What if he laughs at me? Will he think this is a silly high school crush that I have completely blown out of proportion in my head? Is that what it is?*

Deciding that I will never forgive myself if I don't try, I bang loudly on his door and yell out his name before I can talk myself out of it.

Evidently my urgency startles him because when he flings open the door, his hair is sleep mussed and he is standing before me stark naked.

I suck in what is likely half the air in the enclosed hallway as my wide eyes absorb him in all his naked glory. His body is beyond magnificent. My tongue flicks out of its own accord to wet my lips as my gaze lands on his manhood. Even in its flaccid state, it is a sight to behold. When it begins to grow in response to my open perusal and obvious fascination, I force myself to pry my eyes back up to his face.

His expression is bemused, and he makes no effort to cover himself. He is clearly completely comfortable in his own skin. He rests a raised arm on the wide open door and gives me a questioning look. He is obviously wanting to know what is so important that I summoned him unclothed from his slumber, but my mind can't seem to form a coherent thought.

"Oh, ummm," I finally say dumbly.

He doesn't budge nor help me out of the awkward silence that ensues as I search for my words. I consider fleeing, but my feet feel glued to the bright carpet. I sense that this is a monumental moment in my life that I will look back on as either my best choice or my worst. I make a snap decision, figuring that no matter what, I will *not* look back on this and wonder what *could* have been.

Jumping in with both feet, I say, "Can I come in?"

If he's surprised by my bold question, he doesn't let it show. He takes an interminable-feeling moment to look me up and down. I'm dying to know what he's thinking. Without verbally answering, he steps back to widen the door opening. I slide inside to join him, the man from my dreams, in his real-life room.

## 23

The size of his room surprises me. It is larger and nicer than the one I have moved back into, but not as nice as the suite Cam and I had been intended to share. I would have thought that shipboard entertainers would have more modest 'crew-sized' accommodations––possibly even sharing a room with another worker. My eyes are immediately drawn to his King-sized bed, and I can't help wondering if he has already shared it with anyone during this trip.

Despite my brazenness in the hallway, Andrew does the gentlemanly thing and detours into his bathroom before emerging with a plush bath towel wrapped low around his hips. My wayward gaze travels down him, visualizing what I have just seen that is now hidden below the white towel.

He watches my eyes travel down his body, and I see his Adam's apple bob as he swallows. Even though I've given him a fairly open invitation and his body's reaction makes it obvious that he wants me––at least on a physical level––he keeps his distance from me.

When I sit down on his bed, I assume he will join me.

Instead, he walks over to the open sliding glass door and steps out onto his balcony. I don't have to debate long before joining him out there. The cool breeze off the water feels fantastic because the air is still surprisingly humid and warm. We stand there for a moment side by side, looking out over the sea.

It strikes me that I should not be so certain about sleeping with this man that I barely know. Perhaps my fantasies about him have made me feel like I know him, even though I really don't. I'm fairly sure that the reality of a night in his bed will not be able to live up to the frequent imaginings that I have created in my head, but I steadfastly refuse to not find out. I don't want to look back on my life and wonder what might have been.

Choosing to see this through, I place my palm on his bare, sinewy back. Sliding my hand slowly down, I pull the towel that is covering him loose and toss it inside the room. "You won't be needing that." My voice sounds husky.

"What about your husband?" he spits out the last word.

"It's all fake," I promise him.

He turns to face me, warning, "I can't make you any promises about the future."

I am touched that even though I am basically throwing myself at him, he is holding back and trying to protect me. Most men would have thrown caution to the wind and attacked by now. I slowly slide my sundress down my body and let it pool on the ground. "I'm not asking for any promises," I assure him as I enjoy the feeling of his half-lidded, appreciative gaze travelling down my barely-covered skin. His eyes linger on my bare breasts before travelling down to my skimpy, lace panties. He reaches out, rubbing the back of his finger lightly over one of my nipples. It instantly hardens, straining for more.

"You're sunburnt," his observation comes out almost like a question. I had nearly forgotten about my red skin.

Pain is the furthest thing from my mind in this man's presence. "It's okay," I reassure him, touched that even in our current state of undress, he is concerned about my wellbeing.

Evidently unable to restrain himself any longer, Andrew crushes his lips to mine. His kiss is so different than Cam's had been. Even though it is engulfing and probing, it is also mind melding and passionately intense. I get lost in the thrill of it.

We tightly clutch each other––our hands easing down each other's backs. As his tongue slides along mine, I allow my palms to smooth down over his naked butt. I give it a firm squeeze and pull him even closer to me.

We both groan as his now straining, hot manhood presses into my bare tummy. He is hard and ready. Feeling the undeniable evidence that he wants me––physically, anyway––is intoxicating. Unable to resist the magnetic draw of him any longer, I lightly graze my fingertips around to his front––moving my lower-half back slightly to allow easier access to him.

Wrapping my hand loosely around the base of his erection, I lightly stroke his length a couple of times––enjoying the feeling of his warm, velvety smooth skin. He tips his head back, exhaling deeply, obviously relishing my touch.

"I can't believe it's you touching me like this." He lowers his head to look me in the eye.

His words perfectly mirror my thoughts. "I can't believe it's you I'm touching like this," I say aloud, making him smile. "I've wanted you since we were teenagers," I admit, releasing my grip on him to wrap my arms around him.

His face registers utter surprise. "No." The word is part accusation, part question. At my nod, he leans down and kisses my cheek. "You were the dream, Ruthie. You still are."

He kisses his way over to my ear and down my neck as he speaks. "You're gorgeous and sweet and smart and funny."

His words are perfect. I find them hard to believe because it's just too good to be true, but the temptation to let my mind accept them as fact is overpowering. I want to savor this feeling––like I am actually important to this man––even if it only lasts for tonight.

"I'll skip over your poor, red shoulders," he says kindly as he lowers himself and his skilled mouth finds my breast.

My hand digs into his hair, holding him to me as he suckles. My head tips back and my mouth opens of its own accord as his masterful lips and tongue pleasure me. When he kisses his way across to my other breast, he pauses midway to look up at me. I look down and our eyes lock for a moment. His dark hair is adorably mussed and the look he is giving me is one of utter adoration. His eyes are so strange, yet so familiar. I have visualized different sizzling scenarios of this moment in my head so many times that it almost feels like it has actually happened before. The realization that it is truly occurring––not just in my vivid imagination––is beyond thrilling. My knees almost crumple with the intensity of the feelings that flood my system. Having this man of my dreams worshiping my body in real life is almost too much to handle.

He continues his ministrations, and I suck in a deep breath as his lips travel downward. When he pops a smacking kiss on my belly button, I giggle and he grins up at me. All humor is quickly forgotten as his hands slide down my hips and inside my panties. He slips the scant garment down and I daintily step out of them.

Gently turning us so that my back is against the railing, he pauses for a moment looking at me––all of me. I enjoy his open and approving perusal before briefly wondering about the sturdiness of the safety rails. It would be just my luck to lean my weight against the barricade, trusting it fully, only to end up toppling overboard.

Just after deciding that it is worth the likely infinitesimal risk of falling and drowning for the opportunity to be with this man, all coherent thought leaves my brain as he kneels before me to pleasure my most intimate area with his talented mouth. I spread my feet apart and clutch the railing behind me with both hands as this real-life magician works his magic on me.

Allowing my head to fall back, I see the star-filled sky and hear the waves lapping against the slowly moving ship. I couldn't have dreamt up a more idyllic, romantic setting for my tryst with Andrew. Waves of intense pleasure swirl within me as all of my attention shifts to focus on my core.

Crying out in ecstatic release, I forget any worries I previously held about anyone else with a balcony hearing us. Lost in the moment, I can't muster any concern about modesty or shocking anyone else. All that matters is this man, his body, and the surreal feelings he is bringing out in me.

My body pulses to his rhythm, rocking me with the most intense orgasm of my entire life. I shudder as the pleasure rolls through me. When some semblance of rationality begins to return to me, I realize that Andrew is still on his knees, bowed before me. He is looking up into my eyes, watching my facial expressions morph as the thrill of his loving attention washes over me. The enamored look he is giving me is far superior to anything I could have imagined in my dreams of him.

Still reeling from the intensity of my body's reaction to this man, I don't object when he sweeps me into his arms and carries me inside his cabin. I trail kisses along his ear and down his neck while he's walking with me as if I am as light as a feather. After he gently places me sideways across the

ANN OMASTA

bed, I scoot back and watch him. I'm immensely touched when he takes the time to grab a pillow from near the headboard to place under my head.

The pillow makes me comfortable and puts me at the proper angle to ogle him while he makes preparations for our lovemaking. He truly is a magnificent male specimen. Every inch of him is lean and rippling with muscle definition. I'm relieved to see that he has his wits about him enough to think about protection because I am practically incoherent with need.

I don't bother to attempt to hide my fascination with his body as he rips open the foil packet and sheaths himself. His manhood is fully erect, ready to become one with me. I lick my lips in anticipation as his gaze travels down and back up me. I am bare before him––fully exposed and slick with need.

His eyes lock with mine and I can feel my breath coming in quick pants as the anticipation of this moment builds beyond what I would have thought possible. "You're sure?" he asks one last time.

Thrilled by his concern, but unable to speak, I nod my head in answer. That is evidently all the confirmation that he needs because he lithely joins me on the bed, his warm body hovering over me. My legs are spread wide and I can feel his smooth skin at my opening. I raise my hips needing more, but he holds back, the strain evident on his face. I look up at him, ready to plead for mercy––aching with the need to have him inside me.

"I can't believe it's *you*," he tells me before kissing me on the lips.

"I can't believe it's *you*," I mirror his words against his mouth.

He groans, sliding his tongue and cock into me at the same time. I am engulfed by the most intensely pleasurable, mind-numbing sensations imaginable as I wrap my limbs tightly around him, not wanting to ever let go. I can't get close enough to him, and the more I pull him to me, the more of himself he gives. I gaze down the length of him. His strong back muscles undulate as he slides in and out of me. We move in unison, clutching each other's sweat-slicked skin as if our lives depend on our primal mating.

He pumps deep into me, burying himself to the hilt-- hard and fast. I meet him with each stroke, straining for even more of him. Finally, unable to stand the pressure any more, I moan incoherently in sweet release, pulsating around him. He follows my lead, letting go--his hot breath bursts out near my ear as he groans with pleasure.

Staying inside me, he relaxes down on my body. The warm, solid weight of him is exquisite. I could stay like this forever.

I think that he might have fallen asleep, but he surprises me by mumbling near my ear, "Did I hurt you?"

"Hurt me?" I ask him, surprised. "No, that was on the opposite end of the spectrum from pain."

I feel his cheeks move into a smile against me as he gently places his lips on my shoulder. "I meant your sunburn. I didn't intend to get so carried away like that," he reveals.

"What sunburn?" I ask him, only half-teasing. My charred shoulders and thighs had been the last thing on my mind during our sexy tangle. Now that he's mentioned it and reminded me, though, my skin is starting to feel rather hot.

He gets up, and I instantly miss the feel of him on and in me. Making quick work of the condom disposal, he heads into the bathroom. Wondering if I should cover myself, but not having the energy to get up, I stay sprawled across his bed. Insecurities begin to slowly creep their way into my mind as I wonder if he is expecting me to leave. I would much rather spend the night in his bed and in his arms.

When he returns, he has a jar of coconut oil in his hands. "This stuff is supposed to be soothing for burned skin," he informs me.

I'm touched by the thoughtful gesture. Being familiar with the many highly-touted wonders of coconut oil from my visit to Hawaii, I nod at him. "It's also supposedly a wonderful moisturizer and lubricant," At the last word, I give him my best naughty grin and waggle my eyebrows.

"Mmmm," he smiles back at me before rejoining me in the bed. "We better test this out for ourselves to see if it's as great as they say."

## 24

*W*e spend the entire night giving each other coconut oil massages; sliding our limbs over each other's skin in the oversized bed; and tasting, touching, and memorizing every inch of each other's body. It is by far the most glorious, inhibition-free night of my entire life, and one that I am certain I will never, EVER forget.

Daybreak begins peeking over the water through the open curtains all too soon. Although we haven't slept much, I feel more relaxed and rested than I have in months. I stretch luxuriously and savor the fact that Andrew caresses me and snuggles along the length of me in his slumber.

I had been planning to get up early, so I could start to repair some of the damage done by last night's show, but Andrew's embrace makes it too tempting to stay in bed cuddling. I nuzzle into him and doze back to sleep.

The next time I awaken, the sun is high in the sky and I have to use the bathroom. As much as I don't want to leave Andrew's warm, strong arms, staying in bed is no longer an option.

When I get dressed and emerge from his tiny bathroom,

ANN OMASTA

Andrew is still sleeping soundly. Knowing that he had as little sleep as I did, I opt not to wake him. Instead, I sneak quietly out of his room to return to mine.

I am pleased to find the adjoining door inside my room open, and Syd sitting on the couch in the makeup room waiting for me. One look at my rumpled appearance, and he says, "Mmm, Girl...spill. I need details."

Before I can even open my mouth, he holds up his hand with his palm facing me. "Wait," he orders before dragging me into the tiny bathroom and maneuvering us around to close the door. "Now talk," he tells me.

It is impossibly sweet that he wants to protect me from the show's wrath, but I am not ashamed of the night I spent with Andrew. I would do it over again a gazillion times, if given the chance.

Deciding to humor Syd, I stay in the miniscule space. "It was by far the most amazing and passionate night of my entire life," I reveal to him.

He tries to clap with glee, but this water closet isn't really intended for two. He bumps into me as he tries to raise his hands, so he ends up just hopping up and down, saying, "Yay!"

I smile at his obvious enthusiasm. The man seems truly happy for me, and it is wonderful to know that I have someone related to the show who is actually on my side and wants what is best for me.

"So, let me get this straight." He grins down at me when he stops hopping in place. "In the past couple of days you have gotten married to one hot stud of a man, taken the internet by storm..." I start to object to that, but he shakes his head to stop me. "There is no such thing as bad publicity, Darling," he reminds me. "In the last twenty-four hours, you have become a household name."

"For being hated," I insert.

He goes on as if I haven't spoken. "You have rediscovered your high school sweetheart." I start to correct that overly optimistic description, but instead decide to let him finish. "And you've had a night of mind-blowing sex with the super-hot magic man of your dreams."

I nod, admitting that what he has recapped is mostly accurate. "That's a whirlwind of wild activity, even in my crazy life."

"Ooh-whee!" he yells, despite our close proximity. "Can we trade bodies for a little while? I want to be you, Sweets."

I shake my head, grinning at this silly, kind-hearted man. He has somehow managed to make me feel better about the entire situation with the show. I have been focusing on all of the wrong things. So what if I looked bad on one episode? I can easily shift that perception and win over the world.

"I'm not the hateful, spoiled brat they made me look like on the show," I say aloud to Syd, feeling a sudden epiphany.

"Of course not." His brow furrows slightly as if the thought of me being bratty is ridiculous.

"I'm kind and thoughtful and loving," I add.

"You are indeed," Syd affirms.

"I just need that side of myself to be portrayed on the show," I decide. "Once the reality-television-watching portion of the world sees how I feel about Andrew, they'll realize that I'm worth rooting for. And everyone will love Andrew. How could they not?"

I raise my gaze up to Syd, who shrugs his shoulders as if to say he cannot imagine someone not loving Andrew.

"The audience is already behind Cam and Bellamy––Team CamBell. I just have to get the producers to add Andrew to the show, so we can let everyone see how great Team RuRew is!"

"Team RuRew...I love it!" Syd seems sincerely excited. "Go get 'em, Tiger."

Feeling fired up, I turn to open the door and put my plan into action. I'm almost to the hallway door when I hear Syd say, "Hey Babe, you might want to brush your teeth and change out of yesterday's dress before you take over the world."

## 25

Scrubbed clean, and in a fresh dress, I emerge from my room--now ready to win over the world. I head down to the lobby and sense that my luck is already turning around when I spot T.J. near the concierge desk.

I boldly walk over to him, prepared to justify my case and negotiate getting Andrew added to the show roster.

T.J.'s face lights up with fake enthusiasm at my arrival. "Ruthie, darling," he air kisses both of my cheeks.

"I need a favor," I tell him firmly, deciding that he owes me after the way he and his cohorts made me look on the show.

"Anything for you, my dear," the sarcasm is dripping from his voice.

*How did I not see what a complete phony he is before?* I wonder. It is amazing how the chance at fame had blinded me to the obvious.

"Someone from my past is on the ship, and I would like for him to be made a part of the show." The idea that Andrew might not want to be included on the show crosses my mind as the words exit my mouth, but I squelch that fear. *He makes his living on stage, so the extra publicity would have to be good for him, right?*

T.J. blinks a couple of times, pondering my request. "Well, if he's with you, he'll be a part of the show," he says logically. "We just need him to sign a waiver." He gestures to Jamie, who flips pages in her clipboard until she finds what she's looking for and hands the requested paper to me.

I nod and walk away before he changes his mind. That was much easier than I had expected. Now, I just need to convince Andrew that he should agree to be on the show.

Heading straight to his room, I knock on his door before I can chicken out. It takes him a bit to open it, and my breath is taken away as I gaze at him. His damp hair indicates that he is freshly showered, he's still shirtless, and he's handsome as sin.

"Hi," I breathe out, my other words having left me at the sight of him.

"You're back," he smiles before pulling me in for a crushing kiss. "I was afraid you had bolted and that last night was just an epic one-night stand."

That thought hadn't even crossed my mind, but I suppose waking up alone after our passion-filled night of rolling around his bed would make him wonder why I slipped out so quietly. I can't stop the joy from bubbling up over his use of the word 'epic' in reference to our phenomenal night. I felt that way about it, but the confirmation that it was fantastic for him too is life affirming.

He stands back to let me walk through the doorway, and I trail a hand along his taut abs on my way. He sucks in a breath at my light touch, and I am relieved to see that our lust for each other hasn't lessened in the slightest. The rumpled bed catches my eye, and I am tempted to rejoin him there, but the paper in my hand reminds me that I am on a mission.

The smell of bacon lures me out to the balcony, and I am pleased to find a nice room service spread on the tiny side table. I give him a questioning look over the sheer amount of food.

"I was hoping you would come back," he reveals, joining me outside.

I plop down on one of the chairs and swipe a slice of pineapple, but my face falls when I see the open laptop sitting on the other chair. My sister, Roxy's face is frozen on the screen. "You're watching the show?" My voice goes slightly higher at the end, although the question is rhetorical. I don't want him to get a bad impression of me, and I'm utterly embarrassed by the selfish air the show portrays me in.

"I wanted to see what we are dealing with here." He closes the laptop and sets it inside before rejoining me on the balcony.

I am beyond touched that he has referenced what 'we' are dealing with. It makes me feel like he and I are already a team.

Deciding to be completely upfront, I hold the paper out towards him. "I'd like for you to be on the show."

He doesn't take too long to contemplate his decision. "Anything for you," he says as he gets up and takes the paper inside to scrawl his signature.

I just hope he doesn't grow to feel like he has just signed his life away.

$\mathcal{W}$e are now anchored at a tiny, quaint island in the Bahamas, so Andrew and I decide to take advantage of the opportunity to walk around the port. Glancing back at the ship, I am once more astounded by its sheer size. The massive monstrosity dwarfs everything else on or near the island. It makes me wonder about the logistics and equipment required to dig the deep trench that permits big cruise liners entry to the port.

As we walk along the boardwalk towards the shore, I'm surprised to find that I almost feel like the ground beneath me is moving. When I mention the odd sensation to Andrew, he smiles down at me, "You already have your sea legs."

"Umm, great...I guess." I mutter, wrinkling my nose, not at all sure that this is a good thing.

Upbeat Reggae music is being pumped through evenly spaced speakers along our path. The fun tunes make it difficult to stress about anything. Andrew takes my hand and swings me around as our steps begin naturally falling in time to the music. Jake, the cameraman who has been assigned to cover our island excursion, seems to have no trouble walking backwards to capture every moment. I'm in awe of his grace, considering that I would probably fall over my own feet if I attempted such a maneuver.

I am relieved when Andrew mentions that he is doing another shipboard show later this week, meaning he will not be flying home from the island as I had initially feared. When the relaxing and familiar song, "Don't worry, be happy" begins playing, I decide to truly take it to heart and let my troubles melt away.

The pastel colors of the tiny beachside shops are eye-catching and there is a plethora of tiny straw huts with natives selling wares to the tourists from the ship. I have the feeling that the little island comes alive with boisterous activity when a cruise ship filled with people arrives at the dock. The locals probably enjoy the chance to make extra money, but still likely breathe a sigh of relief as the ship sails away leaving them alone on their peaceful slice of paradise.

There is a warm breeze blowing off the ocean that helps ease the heat from the intense sunshine. I am thankful for the gauzy cover-up that Syd presented me with this morning to protect my tender skin from further burning. I'm also wearing the enormous sunglasses the waiter purchased for me.

Stopping at a shopping hut, Andrew purchases me a huge, floppy straw hat with a purple ribbon to provide me further protection from the sun. It perfectly completes my gaudy tourist ensemble.

We spend the entire day shopping, walking along the white sandy beach, splashing in the warm turquoise water, attempting to sneak away from Jake to make-out, failing at giving Jake the slip but making out anyway, eating fresh seafood, looking for shells, and having the absolute best time of my life. I don't want this glorious day to ever end.

Before heading back to board the ship, we decide to make

a quick stop at a shaded hut to sit in high-backed chairs and sip Rum Runners from hollowed-out coconuts. Andrew generously buys one of the icy beverages for our videographer, Jake, so our stalker-for-the-day actually gives us some space and sets down the camera to enjoy it.

I take advantage of the off-camera time to gush a little bit. "This day has been absolutely phenomenal!"

"The best," Andrew agrees, nodding before picking up his coconut. He slides the straw into his lips and makes a silly, puckered sucking face as he draws the delicious icy coolness up to his mouth.

I laugh with him before turning serious. "You are even better than I imagined, and I already figured you were pretty fantastic," I tell him honestly.

"How did I ever let you get away?" he asks, rubbing the back of his finger along my cheek.

I lean into his touch, happier than I ever remember being. Despite knowing that this relationship has been a complete whirlwind, I am unable to keep the hope at bay--maybe, just maybe, I have finally found my happy ending.

That peaceful thought is interrupted by the blaring of our ship's horn.

## 27

*A*fter the ship gives a loud, warning blare of its horn, Andrew, Jake, and I share a panicked look. We all bolt upright—–our eyes bulging in similar looks of alarm.

"Does that mean...?"

I don't bother to finish the question because Jake is already grabbing his camera and making a run for it. "I guess so," Andrew responds, even as he throws money onto the table, waves to the bartender, grabs my hand, and hightails it out towards the pier.

I am wearing high-heeled sandals, so I have to take tiny steps. My legs get in three strides to each one of Andrew's. The shuffle-scurry I am attempting has to look ridiculous, so I'm relieved that Jake is in too big of a hurry to film us. I just hope there aren't any cameramen on the top decks of the ship capturing our tardiness.

"Wait, please wait!" I yell even as I see the aft of the giant ship easing away from the dock. We run to the end of the wooden platform, but it is of no use. The ship sails smoothly past the end of it and out towards the open ocean. It clearly isn't going to turn around for us.

"Well, crap...now what?" I turn to the stunned men standing next to me. They are both giving me wide-eyed questioning looks as if they expect me to know what to do.

Eventually, Jake pulls out his cell phone to make a call—presumably to one of the producers of the show. He walks away from us, back towards the pier entry, likely craving some privacy to blame our missing the ship fiasco on Andrew and me.

I notice for the first time a young man fishing off the end of the pier. Deciding that he must be a native to the island, I ask him about the possibility of finding a hotel room for the night. He shrugs his shoulders and shakes his head, making me think we might be out of luck.

The realization that our passports and other valuables just sailed away on the ship begins to make me feel slightly panicked. We only have with us what we needed for a day at the beach, not supplies for an overnight (or longer) island stay. "We have to get back on that ship," I mumble, thinking out loud.

"You can try the *Pilot*," the teenaged fisherman informs me, "but Cap'n ain't gonna be happy." He raises his arm indicating the small black boat with white lettering spelling "Pilot" that is alongside the cruise ship.

"The *Pilot*, of course!" I feel like kissing the young man, but sense that wouldn't be appropriate. We watch in the distance as the *Pilot's* captain, who has guided the massive cruise vessel out to sea, steps back onto his own much smaller boat before its return to the dock.

I lick my lips nervously as we watch the crew of the pilot boat work to secure the ropes to the pier. "Hi, there!" I give a friendly shout, wiggling my fingers in what I hope is a flirtatious gesture. My uneasiness kicks up a notch when I realize that Jake has ended his phone call and rejoined us with his camera rolling to capture this entire exchange.

The gruff, crusty captain doesn't acknowledge me, but I will not be deterred. "We were hoping you might be willing to help us out." The grouchy, white bearded man still gives no outward signs that he even hears me, but I forge on. "You see, we missed our ship," I start.

At this, he crosses his arms to rest over his plump belly and gives me a weary look. He doesn't utter a word out loud, but his nonverbal communication is screaming, *I've heard it numerous times before, Lady, and I don't care!* His stance indicates that he is clearly annoyed, but I can't back down. We need to get back on the ship.

Evidently deciding that cash is king, Andrew retrieves several bills from his wallet and holds them up in an attempt to tempt the captain into giving us a ride. This earns him a disdainful sneer from the man, who is clearly unimpressed with the bribe.

I'm not overly hopeful that it will work, but I am desperate for his help, so I try mentioning the show. "I'm filming a television show on the ship," I raise a hand towards Jake as verified proof that what I am saying is true, "and we really need to catch up to them."

He raises his eyes to mine, but they are bereft of any concern for our predicament. His cool glare indicates that nothing I can say will convince him to give us a ride out to our sailing away ship.

Seeming to decide that the television angle is our best bet, Andrew jumps in. "Yes, we are both on the show now, actually. It's called *Cruising for Love,* and you can watch it online."

I almost chuckle at his desperate attempt to win over the grumpy man, who clearly wouldn't have any interest in watching our cheesy reality tv show. I nearly fall over in surprise when he squints up at us for a closer look. "Ruthie?" he finally asks.

Amazed that he would have even seen the show, let alone

know my name, I nod in answer. "Where's Cameron?" he asks me after giving Andrew the once-over.

"Probably with Bellamy," I answer flippantly.

"Team CameRu isn't going to work out?" His face looks crestfallen, as if we have just told him someone he cares about is critically ill. I shake my head, shocked that this man--who doesn't appear at all to be our target audience-- is a fan of the show.

He seems to mull over my revelation for a moment before asking, "Are he and that hot red-head really an item?" Before I can answer, he covers his ears with his palms. "Wait...Don't tell me. I don't want to ruin it. I'll just watch the show."

He reaches out a hand to help me on board his boat, and shoos away the money Andrew offers as he climbs aboard, followed by Jake. "We are so looking forward to the next episode of the show. Wait till I tell the wife I met you." He is practically giddy with excitement--a complete about-face from the previous staid grump he appeared to be just seconds ago.

After radioing the cruise ship that we are on our way, he maneuvers the *Pilot* away from the dock and zooms to catch up with our vessel. When we pull alongside the ship, they open a door and drop a ladder for us to climb aboard.

"Thank you so much," I smile at the man who saved the day for us.

"Could I take a picture with you?" He seems almost nervous as he asks the question.

"Of course!" I am thrilled to comply as he holds his cell phone up to take a selfie of us.

He leans in close to my ear after snapping the photo. "I knew you couldn't be nearly as bad as they made you look," he tells me before kissing my cheek.

Unsure how to respond to that, I smile and give him a hug before turning to climb up the scary, rope-lined ladder to our ship. I ignore the appreciative whistle from below, uncertain which of the men looking up at me has done it. I'm guessing my dress is affording them all a full view of my bikini-clad bottom. I just hope Jake isn't capturing the entire crotch shot on video for the world to stream at will.

*A*ndrew and Jake make short work of the flimsy ladder, and the *Pilot* sails away from our ship. The captain makes a big production of blowing me a kiss, which I feign catching and smacking to my lips.

"Super-stardom pays off," Andrew teases near my ear.

Unfortunately, my new notorious status can only take us so far. Standing before us is the same ticket agent who had greeted me when I originally boarded the ship. Judging by the snarky look he is giving me, I can tell that he remembers our previous encounter, and he is not impressed that he has been called back to welcoming duty due to our tardiness in boarding the ship.

Jake presents his ticket, hands over his camera for inspection, and makes his way through the metal detector. Retrieving his camera, he turns it on us.

Andrew hands over his ticket and personal belongings, not seeming to notice that I am holding back. Now it is undeniably my turn, and Mr. Not-So-Friendly is holding out his hand, waiting for my ticket. I hand him my driver's license from my purse, praying that this will be enough.

"Ticket, please," he snaps, dashing my hopes of easy mid-sea entry.

"I still don't have a ticket," I admit before adding, "But don't you remember me from before?"

"Ma'am, there are thousands of passengers on this voyage. I can't possibly remember everyone," he points out nastily. "No ticket, no cruise," he gives me a hateful smile, and I am certain that he remembers me. I want to ask him if he intends to make me walk the plank, but I fear that his answer might be in the affirmative.

"Did you lose your ticket?" Andrew asks, perplexed. "We had to show them with our identification when we disembarked the ship," he prods, evidently trying to make me remember.

"I've never had a ticket," I tell him. "I gave them my ID when we got off. They didn't ask me for a ticket." I can hear the panic starting to surface in my voice.

Just when I'm beginning to wonder if this is some kind of trick that the show has set up to capture on film, Jamie appears. She whispers something in the ear of the man who seems to love being my obstacle. He rolls his eyes, but steps aside to let me pass.

After we decide to get cleaned up for dinner, Andrew leans in to give me a sweet kiss goodbye. We don't want to let each other go. We end up making out in the hallway, until an older passenger clears her throat as she is trying to edge past us to get to her cabin.

"I miss you already," Andrew tells me as he turns reluctantly toward his room.

Jake follows me as I float down the hallway in the opposite direction--giddy with happiness--to my own room.

## 28

*A*ndrew waits for me in the marble entryway to the dining room. Even though we still manage to be the last ones to arrive at the table, being on Andrew's arm makes me not worry about it a bit. I'm no longer consumed with how everything will play out on the screen. Besides, it can't possibly be much worse than how I've already been portrayed.

The presence of Andrew makes everything better. I feel like I have someone by my side who is ready to jump in to defend me, clear up any misunderstandings, and guard my back no matter what.

Bellamy and Cam are fully open with their enamored feelings for each other. Not that they hid it very well before, but now they seem to want the world to know that they are an item. In fact, they have scooted their chairs so close together that they are practically on top of each other. She isn't glaring at me, so I'm guessing Andrew's arrival has helped ease any awkwardness about her relationship with my husband. I hope she has also realized that I'm not nearly as spoiled or evil as the show made me out to be.

Paul and Tiffany are still clearly in the midst of their honeymoon phase. They are practically mooning over each other and totally ignoring the delectable appetizer plates that have been presented to us. I wonder if they will win the prize money since they are apparently the only wedded couple that might still work out.

I feel bad for Josh. He is the only one of the cast who doesn't seem to have any hope of finding love via the show. It might not have worked out as intended for the rest of us, but at least we have love interests. It makes me wonder if he feels left out and lonely. If he is, he gives no outward signs of it. He seems utterly happy-go-lucky, as if he doesn't have a care in the world. Perhaps his intentions behind joining the show leaned more toward the money and fame side rather than the love side of the equation.

I hadn't planned on finding love, but figured it would be a wonderful bonus if I could discover it. I would have never dreamed how things would veer off in a direction so marvelously different from the producer's plan during filming.

If I had been able to write a script for how things would go, I would have been portrayed as a better person on the show that aired, but I would have still found Andrew, and he would be exactly the kind of sweet, thoughtful, funny, sexy, humble, and dreamy man that he is. I smile over at him and he returns my loving gaze. Every time I glance his way, I'm still bowled over that it's really him.

Perusing the menu filled with fancy cuisine choices, like broiled lobster tails, steak Diane, prime rib, and rack of lamb; I am struck with the urge for something a little less heavy and high-end. "You know what really sounds good?" I ask the table at large. After pausing to let them wonder for a moment, I reveal, "A big, juicy cheeseburger and fries!"

The ship's captain looks appalled by my pedestrian

suggestion, but the rest of the heads around the table nod to affirm their agreement with my idea. When the waiters arrive to take our orders, Cam takes the lead. "Burgers, fries, and Coke all around," he tells them loudly.

We all smile and hand over our menus, glad to be having a more 'normal' meal tonight, with the exception of the Captain, who calls one of the waiters aside to order the steak. When the waitstaff bring bottles of ketchup to set around the large table, Stubing picks up the bottle nearest him disdain-fully--as if it is filled with slug-covered turds--and sets it aside. *Someone clearly doesn't know how to relax and cut loose at all*, I decide, but I keep my thoughts to myself. Besides, his fuddy-duddy reaction is already obvious to everyone.

The mood at the table is much more relaxed tonight, with the exception of stuffy Stubing. We laugh and tease each other as we become decidedly more comfortable in each other's company. I hope this friendship and easy camaraderie will be presented on tonight's show, rather than them opting to continue to portray us as competitors who can't stand each other and will do anything to one-up one another.

Unfortunately, that hope might just be wishful thinking on my part...

## 29

*W*e head down to the theatre as a cheerful group, having no idea what the next hour of not-so-real reality television is about to rain down on us. Something deep inside me brings about a feeling of foreboding, but I attempt to squelch it by forcing the premonition to the backburner. For some reason, I don't want to believe the show will distort us into something we are not––even though I have already experienced it first-hand.

The episode starts innocently enough with a quick recap of our beautiful wedding ceremonies and the wild pool party that ensued afterward. There is a quick break for a word from the show's sponsors, and then I see my face flash on the screen.

They do an extreme close-up of me nervously saying, "I do" at the wedding. The scene then cuts to Cam carrying me over the threshold into our bridal suite. When Cam turns to kick the door to our room closed, he smiles and winks at the camera. They have added a cheesy chime sound and his tooth actually sparkles à la the 1950's as if to say, *Excuse me, while we christen our marital bed.*

Andrew shifts uncomfortably in his seat as the seemingly romantic rendezvous plays out on the giant screen. He has let go of my hand and moved his body as far away from me as he can, without leaving the seat adjacent to mine.

I turn to him and whisper, "It's not what it looks like." He nods once in acknowledgment of my words, but I can tell by his aloof body language that the video footage is bothering him.

He's not the only one who is troubled by seeing Cam whisk me into his arms with the insinuation that we are going to share our wedding night bed. The tentative truce that I could feel myself forging with Bellamy is blown out of the water as she leans around Cam to shoot eye daggers in my direction. I'm surprised by her strong reaction because I would have thought she would realize by now that the show's producers skew everything to suit their needs.

The show tonight seems to be focused almost entirely on me, which--before all of this started--I would have thought to be thrilling. The fact that they are portraying me as the slutty villain is rather disturbing, though. Scenes of me appearing to flirt with nearly every man on board the ship begin flashing on the screen.

I see myself laughing and touching Paul's shoulder as we play miniature golf together. Tiffany has magically been cut from the shot, so it appears that I have her husband all to myself--even though she was there with us the entire time.

The show's announcer does a voiceover as Syd and I appear on the screen sneaking into the ladies room together. "Ruthie is off to her next rendezvous," the voice says, insinuating that the two of us have gone in there to indulge in a naughty tryst, when in actuality we only went in there to have a private, camera-free chat.

At this point, I'm not a bit surprised when the camera shows me catching the blown kiss from the pilot boat captain. Scrawled underneath my likeness are the words, "An island paramour?" I'm amazed they bothered to add the question mark, since they seem so determined to show me as a complete hussy.

The show continues in this vein——taking every opportunity to display innocent interactions I have had with men during the trip as naughty rendezvous. By the end, they have made it appear like I am a sex-hungry, man-eater who devours every male in sight. It would be laughable, if it hadn't seemed so believable. Even knowing the truth about each of the scenarios that had been shown, it was easy to misconstrue their meaning when confronted with the creatively edited video footage that had just been live-streamed to the world.

Andrew hasn't looked in my direction since the beginning of the show, and I can practically feel the anger and hurt feelings bellowing off of him in waves. I want to shout at him that what he has seen isn't real, but it is hard to deny something that seemingly has video proof. *How can I expect him to accept my innocence when I have a hard time believing it myself after what we just saw?*

The show finally ends with a teaser clip for the next episode. The announcer says mysteriously, "Has Ruthie already found her next victim?" I'm horrified when the scene cuts to a still shot of my Big-O face.

The camera is pointing down towards the water from one of the top decks of the ship. It is positioned directly above Andrew's balcony where I am splayed out leaning back over the railing, clearly in the throes of ecstasy. Although it is dark, the light from inside the room gives enough of a glow to the picture that my face is easily recognizable. It is obvious that I am naked, even though the side of the ship blocks the lower half of my body from view.

Two tiny stars have been placed over my nipples, allowing me to retain that tiny bit of modesty. I suppose I should be thankful for that small favor, since the show streams on the internet and doesn't have the same restrictions as network television would. I wonder if there is video to go along with the picture and if it will be aired on the next episode. I guess I will have to wait with the rest of the world because the screen goes black.

T.J. jumps up on the stage to give us the early results from the program's release. He is smiling, so I can tell that their plans to utterly mortify and humiliate me are bringing them the desired results. He shakes his head, flashing his crocodile-like grin before saying simply, "We are blowing up the internet."

After a raucous round of cheers and catcalls, the crowd in the auditorium disperses. I feel glued to my seat, even when Andrew bolts up from his chair and out of the theater without speaking a word to me. I try to tell myself that I will be able to straighten all of this out, but it feels overwhelming.

When I picture my friends and family watching tonight's unflattering episode of the show and then seeing that picture of me obviously being the recipient of intense oral pleasure, I want to crawl into a hole and hide for the rest of my life. There are just some things that your parents should not have to see, and this definitely fits that bill. The idea that there might be incriminating video to follow makes me break into a cold sweat.

I sit immobile in my seat as the theatre clears out. Several people come up to chat with the other cast members, but no one bothers to talk to me. I'm sure they are at a loss for what to say. I would be, if the situation were reversed.

Someone plops down beside me and I don't have to look over to know that it is Syd. He is the only one on this ship who believes in me unconditionally and gives me unfailing support. We sit in silence for a long while. When he finally speaks, his words are so perfectly Syd that they make me laugh.

"I'd take having my orgasm face shown to the world over having resting bitch face any day of the week, Honey."

## 30

*A*fter giving Syd a hug and assuring him that I will be okay, I head up to the upper deck for some fresh sea air and solitude. I'm trying my best to keep things in perspective--I might be the most scandalous hussy on the internet right now, but notoriety is a fickle thing and will quickly shine its spotlight on someone else.

If I had known how the show would villainize me, I wonder if I would have agreed to be a part of it. Without the show, I wouldn't have rediscovered Andrew, so I have no doubt that I would have agreed to it, even if I had been given full disclosure.

I know that Andrew was hurt by what seemed like my brazenness on the show. I just hope that he will listen to reason and realize that things are not actually what they appeared to be. He is what matters to me. I just have to convince him of the truth. I'm excited to do just that, but I think it's best to give him some time to cool off. He was obviously hurt by the show's unfavorable depiction of my morals.

Looking out over the front of the ship, I enjoy the warm

breeze coming off the water and blowing my hair back. Bending down to rest my chin on my hands on the railing and look down at the dark ocean, I wonder what mysterious creatures lurk deep below the surface. It cheers me to think that dolphins, turtles, crabs, and stingrays might be frolicking right underneath us, with no regard for the ship passing over them or the pesky problems the people on that ship are having.

"Don't jump." Andrew's voice startles me as I'm peering overboard. He walks up close behind me at the pointy bow of the ship.

I turn to the side, my ear near his mouth. "I thought you were angry with me."

"Syd talked some sense into me," he admits. "I know the show blows things out of proportion and makes things look different than they really are. I just needed a reminder."

I nod, immensely relieved that he is proving to be able to not take the show at face-value. "You're the only one I'm interested in, despite what it seemed like on the show."

"I know," he whispers soothingly near my ear before adding, "and the rest of the world will see it too. We'll get this mess straightened out," he promises.

"They made me seem so horrible," I say sadly, wanting to believe that we will be able to fix things, but not quite able to envision it.

"It's going to be okay," he reminds me, brushing my hair to the side and plying the side of my neck with sweet kisses.

I tilt into his soft lips, basking in his tenderness. "I was afraid you believed it," I admit. "I thought I lost you."

"You can't get rid of me that easily," he assures me. "Besides, Syd threatened to kick my ass if I didn't smarten up and find you to talk through things."

"He did?" I can't stop the laughter from bubbling up.

Picturing slender, gentle Syd trying to bully big, tough Andrew is endearing, yet comical.

"He did," Andrew confirms before adding, "That guy really has your back."

"Yeah, he's the only one," I grumble, even though I feel exceedingly grateful for Syd's loyalty.

"He's not the only one, Ruthie," Andrew informs me. "I want to have your back, your front, and everything in between," he says sweetly, placing his palm over my heart. His lips forge a trail from my ear to my cheek as he says between kisses, "I think I'm falling in love with you."

I turn to face him, in shock. "You...you...you're falling in love with me?" I stammer.

He grins at me, "I've never seen you at a loss for words." My eyes roll at his almost-insult, which makes his grin widen before he closes in to brush his lips over mine. "Yes, I'm definitely falling in love with you. I feel like shouting it to the whole world," he gushes.

"You may have just now told them," I give him a sad smile. At his questioning look, I add, "Who knows where they have cameras."

"I don't care about that," he tells me. "What I care about is you and how you feel."

"I think I've been falling in love with you for a while now," I admit, being intentionally cryptic about how long I have harbored these feelings for him. I don't want to scare him away by revealing my almost-obsession too soon.

"It's fast, and it's crazy, but it feels right," he gushes, and I nod in total agreement with his assessment.

He turns me around to face the water and brings his front to touch my back. We hold our arms out to the side and interlace our fingers, Titanic-movie style. "You make me feel like I am the king of the world, Ruthie."

His words vibrate near my ear making me tingle. "There's

no place I'd rather be than right here in your arms," I reveal to him, and I mean it. My emotions have been all over the place since this trip started, with unbeatable highs and devastating lows, but I feel like we have now gotten to exactly where we are meant to be.

## 31

*I*t starts out as a fairly normal day. Andrew and I devour a massive breakfast on his balcony. I'm wearing one of his soft tee shirts, which is way too big for me. We are both famished from a long night of naked cavorting in his bed. He has delightful sensual tricks up his sleeve that make the magic act in his show seem pedestrian. I should feel tired from a lack of sleep, but I can't bring myself to feel anything but completely satiated and content.

He leans over to give me a deep kiss. I am tempted to get swept away yet again by his touch, but I remind us both, "We aren't safe out here. There are eyes and ears everywhere." I point upward and our gazes both follow the path I am indicating. No cameras are visible, but we aren't willing to risk having another secret video taken of our lovemaking.

I am just getting ready to suggest we go inside for some sudsy fun in his teeny-tiny shower when I notice a boat racing to catch up with us. It pulls alongside us and I peer down at the frantically waving passengers.

"Is that...?" I squint to get a better look. "No, it can't be," I try to convince myself.

"What?" Andrew asks, trying to figure out what I'm alluding to.

"That looks like Baggy, my grandmother," I inform him as I run inside the room to throw on some shorts and head down to sea level to see what is going on.

*S*ure enough, it is my crazy grandmother and her husband. Baggy has frantically waved her arms so much that our ship's crew has radioed up to the bridge to have us idle to see what the commotion is all about.

I smile to myself, thinking that Baggy would probably refer to it as a ruckus-fuckus, which would make my mother (her daughter) scold her for using such a horrible word. Mother would then drop her head and rub her temples, claiming that Baggy's outrageously inappropriate behavior had given her a migraine. I could see the entire scene play out in my mind, and it makes me miss my family immensely.

It is an enormous relief when I see her bluish-gray pin curls appear over the threshold as two deck hands struggle to lift her tiny frame up the swinging ladder. She arrives in her typical outlandish style--waving her arms and yelling about a medical emergency.

Fearing that something really bad is happening, I rush forward. "Baggy, what's wrong?"

"Nothing," she stage whispers to me. "I just wanted them to let me board the ship."

Once the deck hands climb back up, she leans over the railing to wave and yell at her husband in the small boat below. "Bye, Sexy! You'll have to get by without having this hot bod next to you for a night or two." She rubs her hands down the sides of her bony frame as she says this and I almost burst out laughing at the bewildered looks the people milling around give each other.

"Ma'am, you can't stay on this ship." I'm not a bit surprised to see the ticket stickler who always tries to keep me from boarding.

Baggy is not having any of his snootiness. "My ride is already gone." She points to the quickly disappearing boat she arrived on.

"He needs to turn around and come get you." He is already raising his radio in an attempt to call back the boat when Baggy starts toward him, her gnarled finger pecking him in the chest. Even though Baggy is more than a foot shorter than him, the man backs up as she reads him the riot act.

"You don't tell me where I can and can't go, young man. I'll take you over my knee and give you a good swat for being an obstinate brat. My medical emergency seems to have cleared up." She turns to give me an exaggerated wink before turning back to him. "That doesn't mean I shouldn't stay here for monitoring. I'm an old woman...we wouldn't want to take any chances."

He seems unsure how to respond to her, like so many others before him. When he remains quiet, Baggy adds another line of reasoning. "Besides, don't you know who I am? My granddaughter needs me, so I am here."

Comprehension dawns on his face at her words. He turns directly to me. "I assume *this* is yours?" he sneers.

I nod, smiling. Feeling overwhelmingly grateful for the presence of my wild, wonderful, and wacky grandmother.

He snarls at us, but flits away without pushing the issue further.

"Baggy!" I hold my arms open and engulf the tiny woman in a hug. She smells like talcum powder and lemon drops. I take a deep breath to savor her soothing, familiar scent. Even though the ship hasn't been gone long, it feels like an eternity

ANN OMASTA

because so much has happened since we left on our voyage. "How are you here?" I ask her excitedly.

"We were on an island not too far from here," she turns directly towards Jake's camera and stage whispers the word, "*spying.* When I saw how they are making you look on that show, I decided to come set them straight. I could tell everything was all hay-wonkers."

She leans in to my ear as if telling me a secret, but still talks loud enough for everyone around--including the cameras--to hear what she is saying. "Are you really sleeping with all of those men, Honey? Because, if so, way to go!"

"No, Baggy, of course not." She looks a little disappointed at my denial, but nods her head in acceptance. At some point, Andrew arrived because he is now standing by my side. I put my arm around him and say to Baggy, "Actually, I only have eyes for one man. Baggy, this is Andrew Stark."

He holds his hand out to shake Baggy's, but she instead offers her hand for a kiss. He obliges, but Baggy is frowning. I can almost see the wheels turning in her head, and I hope she doesn't say anything to give away my ginormous, decade-long crush on Andrew.

"Andrew Stark," she says quietly, mulling it over with her watery eyes squinting up at him. I am able to see the moment the light bulb comes on in her brain. She snaps her fingers. "Aren't you the young man Ruthie has been mooning over since she was in high school?"

Appalled by her lack of couth, I can feel my cheeks burning red with embarrassment. Andrew turns to me, clearly surprised by my grandmother's revelation. I scoff and shake my head as if to imply that Baggy is crazy, which is actually the case.

Not willing to be deterred that easily, Baggy continues. "Yeah, he's the one you danced with at prom, right?"

I don't want this conversation to go any farther, and I can

146

only think of one way to distract Baggy. "I think the bar is already open. Shall we go check it out?"

Like a dog spotting a squirrel, Baggy is instantly interested and alert. "Oh, yes! Lead the way," she tells me, and I hope the topic of my borderline-insane crush on Andrew is dropped for good.

*W*e imbibe a little too much at the poolside bar, but the sun is shining and the frozen beverages are cool and delicious. Baggy has talked the bartender into making us something called Voodoo slushies. I wasn't listening when Baggy prattled off the required ingredients, but I can tell they contain ice, a splash of fruit juice, and a whole lot of rum.

It is obvious that I am getting tipsy when I start attempting to describe the alcohol content in our drinks. "They're rumtastic. Wait...is that a word? How about rumdilicious? Or rumified? Rumrific?" Andrew and Baggy are looking at me like I have lost my mind. So, I settle for, "Super rummy."

As the sun rises higher in the sky, I move my chair to hide in the shade, not wanting to get any more exposure on my still-sensitive skin. Baggy sits right out in the full sunlight after donning enormous fuchsia sunglasses with crystal bling and declaring herself to be "Ready for her close-up."

I smile, knowing that she is going to be an absolute hit on the show. When Jamie asked her to sign a waiver allowing them to film her, Baggy scrawled her signature with a giant heart around it before telling Jamie to have her people call her people so the two of them could "do lunch." Jamie didn't acknowledge the request.

The world will be drawn to Baggy. She is so shocking and

ANN OMASTA

outrageous that they will see no other option except to love her––like the rest of us.

We spend the day sitting at the bar and getting drunk. I tell Andrew about some of Baggy's sillier antics, knowing that this will play really well on the show. *It's about time they use some favorable footage of me*, I decide.

"This one time," I start in on the next story, touching Andrew's arm, "Roxy and I both had chicken pox. We were bored and itchy and miserable. It had snowed the night before, but Mother wouldn't let us go out to play. Baggy came over and made a silly upside down snowwoman in front of our window. She put a blonde wig on her and even gave her boobs!"

Baggy howls with laughter over her own shenanigans. "Oh, I am a hoot!" She shakes her head as if she can't believe how ornery she can be.

It's quiet for a moment as we are all lost in our own thoughts. Baggy raises her crooked pointer finger to waggle at me. "Just remember one thing, young lady," she tells me seeming serious. I'm almost scared to hear what is coming next, but I widen my eyes, silently asking the question. "You are only here on this great earth because I got lucky one night a long time ago!"

Andrew and I both cringe at that unwanted mental image, but Baggy cackles so loudly at her own joke that they can probably hear her up on the bridge. Eventually, we have no choice but to join her.

## 32

*J*ust when I started to think that things might be turning in my favor, another bombshell is dropped. We are sitting at dinner, and I'm feeling refreshed and still a little tipsy.

Baggy had gone with me to my room to nap and cleanup. She and I tried to doze in my tiny bed. It is fortunate that we had so much to drink earlier because her snoring was loud enough to raise the roof on our tiny cabin. I covered my ears with my pillow and passed out, after deciding that in order to get any sleep when I'm not drunk, I'll need to sleep in Andrew's cabin while Baggy is here. I drifted off thinking that I am perfectly okay with that stipulation.

Syd had awoken us by tapping (then banging when we ignored him) on the connecting door to the make-up chamber. He was kind enough to get Baggy camera-ready as well, and the two of them had become fast friends.

I was pleasantly surprised when we arrived at the Captain's table for dinner that they had already added a chair and place setting for Baggy. Someone around here sure seems to keep track of details to make sure everything runs smoothly. My money is on clipboard-carrying Jamie. She definitely looks the part.

We are just digging into the salad and dinner rolls when the crocodile bares his teeth. I can tell by T.J.'s smile that whatever is making him so happy will likely not be in my best interest. He taps his glass with his fork before announcing, "Good news..." He pauses for dramatic effect, during which I stew, knowing that this declaration is bound to be the opposite of good for me.

"We've had a lot of surprising twists come to our attention." He flashes his white teeth as he looks around the table to make eye contact with each of us. The resulting effect of his gaze makes us shift uncomfortably in our seats, like when the preacher stares at you from the podium. *Is he looking at me? What have I done? What does he know?*

Baggy is the only one who keeps stuffing her roll in her mouth, oblivious to, and utterly unaffected by, his words. The rest of us shift our eyes to each other wondering who will be on the grill tonight. I hope it isn't me again. It should be someone else's turn, right?

"Since that is the case," he finally continues, "the last fifteen minutes of tonight's show will be live!" He says this like we should all be incredibly excited about it. Baggy starts a little whoop of enthusiasm before she has a chance to gauge the reaction of the rest of us. Once she sees our concerned and downcast faces, the yelp of excitement peters out into a questioning squeak.

Silence prevails at the table for a long while. T.J. resumes eating as if he has just blessed us with magnificent news that we should all feel grateful for. The rest of us sit there staring at our plates. My stomach churns with the unknown. Deciding that no one else is going to ask, I inquire, "Why are we going live?"

As much as I hate how they cut the film in the editing

room to make me look like a total heel, I'm much more concerned about tripping, saying something stupid, or throwing up a sticky glob of Voodoo slushie on live streaming television. Croc looks up as if he is taken aback by my question. It appears that he really thought we would be happy about this unexpected, new development.

He smiles, this time without teeth. His dark skin makes the whites of his eyes pop. He looks right at me and says mysteriously, "You'll see."

The uneasy feeling I had been fighting increases ten-fold. I *know* that whatever they are planning to reveal tonight doesn't bode well for us. The others seem to sense it too, with the exception of Baggy, who has gone back to loudly crunching her spinach salad, seeming oblivious to the jittery nerves around the table.

When she takes a sip of her iced tea, she shivers in mock disgust. "Blech, that's sweet tea. It has WAY too much sugar for me." She wrinkles her nose in distaste, and a waiter rushes forward to apologize. He quickly scurries off to get her an unsweetened tea. Before he can run back with her fresh glass of tea, she is slurping her straw in the ice at the bottom of the sweet tea glass––having sucked down the entire beverage that she supposedly didn't like. Shrugging her tiny shoulders, she says, "I guess it wasn't *that* bad."

We don't have the energy to laugh at her, even though she is a total nut. I just hope the sugar doesn't make her hyper during the live show tonight, and yes, I am aware that it sounds like I'm worrying about a toddler rather than an old woman. Her age doesn't negate my fears, due to her overarching lack of maturity. *Maybe she'll pull some wild stunt that will keep any negative attention from the rest of us*, I decide as I realize that for the first time in my entire life, I *don't* crave the spotlight.

. . .

*A*ll too soon, dinner is over and it's time to head up to the theatre. The show's cast had barely been able to touch our dinners, with the exception of barely-tipping-the-scales-at-one-hundred-pounds Baggy, who had wolfed down two entire lobsters. Shiny, melted butter had dripped off her chin and onto the plastic bib protecting the royal blue dress Syd had chosen for her. Again, we probably would have found it funny, had we not all been so stressed about the live show.

I am pleased to find when the taped portion of the show begins that they seem to be showing us all in a more favorable light. Andrew is prominently featured with me, and the romantic music and clips clearly indicate that we are a couple. Thankfully, they don't seem to be playing dirty by airing the video of our sexual encounter on his balcony—unless they are saving it for later, which is a constant fear in the back of my mind as we watch.

It appears that this episode won't be focused as much on me as the last one, when the next segment features Cam and Bellamy playing on the beach at our island stopover, sipping from the same glass at the pool, and watching the sunset over the bow of the ship. Their clip is fun, upbeat, and they both look gorgeous. They beam at each other when it finishes and we break for a commercial.

Tiffany and Paul appear on the screen and their portion of the show continues in the same vein as the previous one. They appear happy and in love.

Even Josh, who should feel like the odd-man-out is shown enjoying the ship's amenities and relaxing by the pool by himself, seeming perfectly content.

It's all starting to feel a little 'happily ever after' for reality television. It makes me wonder what kind of bombshells are going to be dropped during the last portion.

I don't have to wonder too long because the show takes a break with a voice-over teaser that we will be live when we return. A flurry of activity begins. Seven chairs are brought out on stage in front of the big screen for the 3 married couples and Andrew. Baggy seems somewhat affronted to not be included in this part of the show, but I am proud of her for not pitching a hissy fit. Syd moves up to sit beside her, so his nearness distracts her from being too upset.

The show comes back and there we are on the enormous screen. It's a little surreal to be sitting in front of a giant version of myself, so I focus my gaze on Baggy in the front row to help ease my nerves.

T.J. walks on stage and makes a big deal about us airing live from the ship. My jittery nerves make me want to shout at him to get on with it, but I force myself to be patient. Besides, if they are getting ready to ruin our lives, I'd prefer to drag it out anyway. *Maybe the ship will capsize or something. Never mind the fact that it has been flat calm seas during our entire voyage...tidal waves can happen, right?* I shake my head slightly, not believing that the show has frazzled my brain so much that I am actually wishing for a tidal wave. *That is messed up.*

Building the intrigue, T.J. teases that ours is a ship filled with secrets. He walks over to Josh and places a hand on his shoulder. "Josh, would you like to spill your secret before the world sees it?"

I'm sure Josh has no idea what they know. How could he? He shakes his head, so T.J. indicates to the production team to roll the video footage. Turning my head back to the screen, I see a giant movie of Josh and Syd with their arms wrapped around each other in a serious lip lock on the top deck of the ship. It is dark, so they probably thought they were alone and didn't count on the ever-rolling cameras.

A murmur of surprise rolls through the theatre audience.

I hear Baggy turn to Syd and say, "Oh, you're a gay. Too bad." I cringe at her word choice as she shakes her head, "You look super hot on the big screen. I could rock your world if you decide to give up on dongs."

I turn my attention back to the announcer, hoping that Baggy's voice wasn't picked up by the live feed. Probably not wanting to give the microphone to Josh after outing him on live television, T.J. moves on to his next victim.

"Tiffany," his voice sounds kind, but I'm sure his attention doesn't bode well for Tiffany, who shifts uncomfortably in her seat. "Did you really think we wouldn't find out your secret?" he asks her, somewhat condescendingly.

She already has tears pooling in her eyes, obviously knowing what is coming. She turns to Paul, "I was going to tell you, I promise."

The video goes to a split shot. Half is zoomed in on Paul's stunned face, while the other half shows a video of Tiffany playing in the park with her nine-year-old son.

T.J. moves in on Paul. "Paul, tsk tsk tsk. Are you disappointed that Tiffany wasn't completely honest with you?"

"Well, yeah, a little...I mean it's a big surprise," Paul stammers.

"Do you think it's as big of a surprise as Tiffany will get finding out that you are a convicted felon?" T.J. asks dramatically as a video of Paul's mug shots and a description of his numerous arson convictions are read aloud.

Tiffany and Paul both appear to be in shock. They are staring straight ahead as T.J. moves over to Bellamy. He gives her a fake smile before saying, "Do you want to tell them or shall I?"

Bellamy gives a slight shake of her head. The color has completely drained from her face, so it is obvious that she doesn't want the world to know whatever is about to come.

Not caring a lick for what she might want, T.J. says, "Bellamy...or should I say, Cinnamon? How long has it been since you turned tricks?" A picture of Bellamy in a barely-there mini skirt, cleavage-baring tank, and cropped burgundy wig appears on the screen. She looks different, but it is obvious that the photo is of her.

Looking down the row of devastated faces, I feel sick for what T.J. is doing to these people who have become my friends. They might have some mistakes from the past or things they don't necessarily want broadcasted to the world, but they are good people. They don't deserve this embarrassment and shame the show is trying to make them feel.

Having done his damage to Bellamy, T.J. sets his sights on Cam. "Cam, Cam, Cam..." Croc shakes his head as if he can't believe what he is about to say. "You seem like you have it all, don't you?" Cam doesn't respond to the rhetorical question. "Do all of the ladies you woo know that you are in debt up to your eyeballs? Keeping up the façade is expensive, isn't it?" T.J. feigns sympathy. "Is that why marrying wealthy women has become a habit for you?" The video clip proceeds to show a montage of eight angry women all claiming that Cam had seduced them into marriage and bled them dry of money before moving on to his next victim. "Interesting tidbit," T.J. chimes in when the women finish their tirades, "That last lovely lady claims that she never filed the divorce papers, so the two of you are still legally married. So, on top of everything else, you became a polygamist when you married poor, sweet Ruthie during your...was it your ninth?...wedding ceremony."

The lump in my stomach flip-flops when T.J. refers to me as 'poor, sweet Ruthie.' I figure any kindness from him is in preparation for the cold-blooded snake to strike. When he moves toward me, I can feel my hands breaking out in a clammy sweat. *What is he going to reveal about me?* I'll have to wait to find out because when he gets beside me, he says, "I'm too upset by all of these shocking revelations to continue. Let's take a break and come back with Ruthie after these messages from our sponsors."

I can barely breathe through the anxiety. *I don't have any secrets, do I?* My only secret was Andrew, and he is here, so that seems a little anti-climactic. *Why did they save me for last? Are they going to tell him about the school picture of him that I've saved all of these years? That is embarrassing, but doesn't seem quite as earth-shattering as some of the juicy tidbits that have already been revealed. Will Andrew be uncomfortable with me once he finds out I have secretly liked him since we were teenagers?*

*Or do they have some other secret they think they know about me? They could probably say almost anything they want to and, even if I deny it, I'll look guilty. Is that what happened with the others? Did they realize that denying their accusations would only make them look guiltier?* I lean out to glance down the row at my co-stars. They are all wearing similar pale-faced looks of shellshock. My gut is telling me that the secrets revealed about them are all true. I feel bad for them. They have had their dirty laundry aired for the world to see. It's not fair. I wish I could rewind the last ten minutes and give them back their privacy.

I turn to give Andrew a sad smile, and he grins back before taking my hand in a show of unity. He has to be wondering what bombshell will be dropped about me. They must think it's shocking to have saved me for the end. As the music for the show starts, my mouth feels like I have just swallowed a wad of cotton. I lick my parched lips and fidget nervously in my seat.

T.J. appears behind me, but I remain facing forward, not wishing to make eye contact with him. "And we're back, with one original cast member left for us to get to know better: Ruthie!" He says my name enthusiastically, like we are great friends as he places a hand on my shoulder. I want to shrug it off, but force myself not to while the cameras are capturing my every move.

"Your co-stars have some shocking skeletons coming out of their closets, don't they?"

I'm not sure why he is asking me this or what he expects me to say. Despite my nerves, I want to stick up for my friends while I have the opportunity. "Everyone probably has something they wouldn't want the entire world to know," I start, but he starts talking before I can add, 'including you.'

T.J. evidently senses and doesn't like where this is heading because he cuts me off. "Indeed. And what about you, Ruthie?" He asks in his smooth and sleazy show-host's voice.

"What about me?" I ask, sounding much more snappy and confident than I feel. My mind is whirling, trying to figure out what they think they know. I smile in the camera's direction, in an attempt to seem calm.

"Nothing to admit before the video rolls?" the slimeball asks.

That's when it hits me. He is fishing for clues. They must not have anything of substance. "Not a thing." I flash a winning smile at the camera now, feeling much more confident.

"It's true," T.J. raises his shoulders as if he is stumped and barely able to hide his disappointment. "We didn't dig up anything too scandalous about you, Ruthie. The only interesting thing that we found out about you is your long-time crush, Andrew." He sweeps his hand out to make sure the audience realizes we are talking about the man on the other side of me.

T.J. puts a hand to his mouth as if he is telling the audience a great secret. "She has kept a photo of him from high school all of these years," he stage whispers. Then he holds up his thumb and pointer finger to indicate the size of the tiny picture.

Andrew squeezes my hand, and I turn to him. The look he is giving me isn't appalled or frightened at all. It's actually one of unbridled adoration. The ice chunk in my tummy melts from his warm gaze. I had been so afraid of my obsessive crush being revealed. Now that it has, the man in question looks amused and happy. Sweet relief floods my system as Andrew and I continue holding hands and presenting a united front.

"So, Ruthie, I guess you win by default." I suck in air, but struggle to hear what else he is saying. "The others have all misrepresented themselves and broken the terms of their contract."

I cringe as he goes down the line, calling each person out for public shaming. "You didn't mention that you are gay," he says to Josh. "Your application said you didn't have any children," he stares down at Tiffany. "I don't recall anything being listed under felonies on your application for the show, Paul." He moves down the row to Bellamy. "I'm the most surprised by you, Dear," he says in his syrupy voice. "I really thought you were destined for stardom." Moving on, he shakes his head. "Cam, someone who has been married eight times and is still married to the most recent one does not get to check the 'single' box on any form ever again."

He moves in front of me. "That leaves you, Ruthie. We didn't find any misrepresentations or outright lies on your paperwork. So, you are the only one of the original six to still be eligible for the money," he informs me.

My breath is coming in shallow pants. That prize money will change my life. Andrew and I will be able to buy a home or travel or start a business or donate it to causes we believe in or do any number of things. That much cash is a game changer and will set us up for whatever we want in life.

I turn to smile at Andrew in my excitement, but he is facing forward. Our hands are still tightly interlaced, but I sense a subtle change in his demeanor. Maybe it just hasn't sunk in with him yet that we will have this much money. I smile to myself because it doesn't even cross my mind to not share the windfall with Andrew. He and I are a team now-- an unstoppable, unbeatable team.

I'm busy daydreaming about all of the wonderful things we can do with the money when I realize that T.J. is still yammering. I manage to focus my attention on the croc as he rubs his chin seeming to deeply contemplate something. "You know, it just doesn't seem like an exciting ending to our action-packed show." He pretends like he is just coming up with all of this, but I'm confident he has it all carefully orchestrated and planned out in advance.

"It's so much money...a quarter of a million dollars," he continues as if he is still mulling things over. "It doesn't seem right to just hand it over to someone simply because her competition was disqualified. That's anti-climactic, and I won't stand for it. We need more of a challenge than that."

"Let's see," he paces dramatically back and forth as if he is frantically trying to come up with something so he doesn't have to hand over an enormous check to me. "The only rules in this game are that there are no rules. I get to make the rules," he adds with a gleam in his eye, and I sense that he is about to reveal whatever challenge I will need to face to win the money.

"I've got it," he holds up a finger indicating his aha moment. "It's a lot of money, Ruthie. In fact, it's enough money to completely change your life, but it doesn't seem fair that you should get both love AND money. So, you need to make a choice," he informs me, "Andrew or $250,000?"

"Now let's be clear here," he interjects before I can say anything, "you don't get both. You have both signed contracts that stipulate you will agree to our terms. Our terms are that if you take the money, you have no further contact with

Andrew after tonight. We will take the money back and sue you for damages if we should find out the two of you are sneaking around behind our backs. I think the others on this panel," he sweeps a hand out to indicate the rest of the group, "can attest to our snooping capabilities."

"So, what will it be, Ruthie...love or money?"

I don't even have to ponder my answer. The money would be great, but we can always make more of that. There will never be another Andrew. I haven't been able to get over him in the years since high school, so I'm certain I would never be able to get over losing him after all we've now been through together. I say the words loudly and clearly, "I choose love."

T.J. turns to the crowd with his mouth open in mock amazement. "Well, folks, I am stunned. I thought for sure that one was going to go the other way. Didn't you?"

Baggy and a few others yell, "No!" Some people clap and others whistle and cheer. I have apparently finally won over the audience.

"Love wins over money." T.J. is shaking his head as if he truly can't believe it. Then, as if he has forgotten something, he holds up his pointer finger. "Wait, there's one person on stage we haven't spoken to." He wheels around on his heel to face Andrew.

"Andrew," T.J. says his name, but gives me a snide look. I can tell by the gleam in his eye during the dramatic pause that I am not going to like whatever is coming one bit. Finally, he speaks, "We brought you onto this show to win Ruthie's heart, and it looks like you have succeeded, my man."

The blood is rushing in my ears. *Andrew was a plant by the show's producers. They brought him here to seduce me. Everything that I have built up in my head about us being in love is built on a lie. It was all completely fake on his part.* This version of reality is too difficult to comprehend. Everything seems to be moving in slow motion as I try to make sense of the harsh truths I am being presented with. I am aware that my body is shutting down, but I don't know how to stop it. The spotlights are swirling and the world is spinning in disarray as I feel myself falling to the ground.

## 33

*I* vaguely remember waking up and feeling safe with Syd carrying me in his arms. The next recollection I have is of a helicopter landing on the ship's helipad before whisking Baggy and me away to an airport. Baggy had me take a sleeping pill before the flight, so things are hazy about the rest of the trip home. The next time I become fully awake and aware of my surroundings, I am safely ensconced in my own bed at home. Baggy is sitting up next to me, watching *Family Feud* at a volume level that could easily be heard across town.

She yells at the television, "Titties! Why aren't you guessing titties?"

When I sit up to see what in the world she is talking about, she turns to look at me, seeming startled that I'm awake. "Oh, hi, Sweets. These morons are driving me crazy...the question is to name a body part that starts with the letter T, and they will *not* say titties."

She seems completely appalled that they aren't listening to her through the tv. "Umm, I don't think they can say that word on television, Baggy," I inform her as she finds the

162

remote and clicks off the set, grumbling about idiots that censor her television viewing.

Finally, she turns her full attention to me. "How are you feeling? Better?"

I nod in answer.

"Good. Everyone has been so worried," she informs me, picking up her cell phone as if that provides proof. There is only one person who I really want to know if he has called, but I hate myself for caring. He sold me out, yet he's still the first person I want to speak with. I can't just shut off feelings I have had for so many years––especially not now that I know the man that teenaged-heartthrob turned into. Well, I thought I knew that man, until I learned of his betrayal.

"Did I pass out on live tv?" I ask my grandma when the fuzziness begins to fade.

"You sure did!" She says it like it's something to be proud of. "Your eyes rolled way back in your head like you were possessed, then you slithered down to the floor like a snake. Didn't hit your head on the chair or anything. It was an excellent blackout. If I ever pass out on television, I hope I do it just like you did...super slow and slinky-like."

I can't believe that she's proud of me for my mad fainting skills, but I guess if I'm going to do it for all the world to see, I might as well do it with finesse.

I don't want to ask the burning questions that are most prevalent in my mind, but I *have* to know the answers. "What did Andrew do when I fainted? Is he still on the ship? Did he win the money? Has he called? Is he never allowed to see me again?"

"Whoa, whoa, whoa, here. Let's back this little red Corvette up a little bit. You are worried about the traitor who came on the show to seduce you and take your money?" Baggy looks disgusted with me.

"No, I just...it's not that...well, yes," I finally admit, feeling ashamed by my weakness, but still needing to know the full story about Andrew. "Just because his feelings for me were fake and staged by the producers of the show, doesn't mean that mine weren't real--very real. Knowing that he lied to me hurts deeply, but it doesn't mean I can just turn off my feelings for him like that." I snap my fingers.

"Hmph," she grumbles before saying, "I really don't know what happened. I called for the helicopter and had Syd carry you to the med center on the ship. You kept waking up and shutting back down, like your body refused to let your mind grasp what had happened."

I decide that sounds about right because I don't remember being in the medical center at all. I hope the cameras weren't recording the entire fiasco. I wouldn't put it past the producers of the show to put together and air a "Cruising for Love--Fainting Debacle" episode.

"Several people kept coming to the physician's cabin to check on you, but we sent them all away," she informs me. She seems to be debating saying something. Evidently making her decision, she adds, "Including Andrew."

I feel my face light up at this news. I can't help myself. As much as I want to be angry with him and not care what he thinks or does, I just can't seem to give up hope. I've felt too strongly about him for too long. My heart wants to believe that there has to be some plausible explanation for what he has done, although my mind can't muster a believable or excusable one.

Baggy seems to want to set my mind at ease that she protected me from Andrew. "I went all grandmama bear on that louse," she informs me. "I told him to stay away and that he doesn't deserve you."

I try to hide the disappointment on my face because I know that her reaction had arisen from a place of love and that she had my best interests at heart. I do wish that she had at least listened to what he had to say, though. Some hopelessly optimistic side of me desperately wants to believe that Andrew had a good reason for what he did and that he is worthy of my love.

Baggy's milky blue eyes light up with an idea. "We could watch the show to see what happened after we left!"

I'm not sure why I hadn't thought of that. Perhaps my mind still isn't quite firing on all cylinders. "Yes!"

I can hardly stand the wait as she goes to retrieve my laptop and pulls up the website. Eventually, she gets the show going, but she seems content to watch the entire thing through from the beginning.

Not having the patience for that, I grab the computer from her. "We already know what happens during this part." I fast-forward all the way to the last couple of minutes. Watching it as an outside party like this, I can see the guilt creep into Andrew's eyes when I say that I choose him over the money. *At least he has some remorse.*

Baggy mumbles some vulgar curse words when T.J. reveals on the screen that Andrew has been playing the game from the beginning. I watch myself pass out in slow motion. Baggy had been right...it was a graceful dismount from my chair, considering that I was not awake.

"Excellent fall!" Baggy tells my limp body on the screen.

A flurry of activity begins as people rush forward to help me. Andrew looks really worried, but Baggy shakes her finger at him until he backs away. I can't tell what she is saying because she's not wearing a wireless microphone like the rest of us, but I have a pretty good guess at the gist of her words.

For as slender as Syd is, he picks my dead weight up from the floor effortlessly. Baggy parts the crowd and leads the way as Syd carries me away to get medical help.

*This is where the show should get really interesting*, I decide as I lean in to see what happened next.

T.J. looks stunned for a moment, but he quickly recovers. "Okay," he starts. "We will post an update on Ruthie's condition on the website." Turning to Andrew, who looks utterly stunned, T.J. says, "We only have a few seconds left. You completed your mission, Andrew. Ruthie chose you over the money, which means you win the money––as long as you stay away from Ruthie. How does it feel to be a very wealthy man?"

The shot closes in on Andrew. His mouth is hanging open and his eyes are staring straight forward as if he can't believe everything that has just happened. "It feels...I feel..."

The screen goes dark indicating the playback is over before we hear what he said. "What?? No!" I yell at the computer. "How could they just leave us hanging like that?" I ask Baggy.

She shakes her head. "I don't know, but it sure does make for riveting television."

$\mathcal{I}$ examine the entire web site, but can't find what I'm looking for. It indicates that I am at home resting and recuperating, but it says nothing about Andrew or the next episode of the show. It's like they have just ended it, leaving the world (especially me) with this huge cliffhanger of how Andrew feels.

I am tempted to throw my laptop across the room, but since I'm still making payments on my credit card for it, I manage to stop myself. Besides, that kind of outburst would only feel good for a second. I'm proud of myself for realizing that in time to curb my destructive instinct. There was a time––not too long ago––when I would have pitched a hissy fit, without any concern for the consequences.

Baggy forces me to get up and take a shower, even though all I want to do is stay in bed. I know that I need to get on with my life, but I'd rather take a little while to marinate in my own misery. No-nonsense Baggy calls that hogwash before ordering me to "suck it up, Buttercup."

I do feel marginally better once my body is clean, and I am sitting upright in a kitchen chair sipping from a mug of

167

pomegranate green tea Baggy has brewed. Baggy reaches over to pat my hand and, in a rare serious moment, she assures me, "It's all going to work out for you, Ruthie. You just wait and see."

As if the universe has heard her declaration, a knock sounds at the door. My face immediately perks up. *Andrew!* His name pops into my mind, but I manage to keep my mouth from uttering it out loud.

My heart pounds forcefully in my chest as Baggy jumps up to answer the door. When I hear a male voice, I can't keep from practically running to the living room to see him.

I stumble to a stop. "Oh... Hi, Syd." I struggle to keep the disappointment out of my voice. I'm happy to see my wonderful friend, but he isn't who I had been hoping was here.

Giving him a warm hug, I realize I must not have been successful in hiding my disillusionment when Syd asks near my ear, "Were you hoping for someone else?"

I shake my head in denial, but can't say anything for fear that the burning ball of misery in my throat will turn to tears.

"It's okay," he tells me, pulling back from our embrace. "No time for feeling sorry for yourself," he informs me sternly. "We only have fifteen minutes to get you camera-ready."

"Camera-ready? Why?" My mind is already abuzz with the possibilities. *Did Andrew choose love over the money and they are coming to tell me? Or are they coming to record my reaction to finding out he took the money without a second thought about me? Or is it some other crazy twist with this unpredictable show?*

Syd has brought a train case filled with beauty supplies that he is now expertly applying to me. I fully trust this man now and don't even bother to watch his ministrations in the mirror as the thoughts and fears about what the show might be up to zing through my brain.

"Are you going to fix me too?" Baggy asks Syd.

"You are always camera-ready, lovely lady." Syd bends down to give her a sweet peck on the cheek after his kind words.

I can't be certain, but I think Baggy's cheeks actually turn pink from his doting. *Is it possible that she's not quite as bold and outrageous as she seems to be?*

I don't have long to worry about that because just as Syd pronounces me to be "perfection," a loud pounding on the door startles us all.

Unable to hide my hopeful enthusiasm, I jump up and jog to answer it. Swinging it wide open, I stumble back a step and say, "Oh, it's you." My voice sounds flat and disappointed, even to my own ears. *Why had I let myself hope that Andrew might be coming for me?*

The croc smiles broadly at me. "It's me," he confirms. "May I?" he asks, indicating that he would like to be invited inside.

I'm tempted to deny him access, but decide I should hear him out. He sweeps into my tiled entryway followed closely by Jake, my favorite cameraman. The red button is flashing on the video recorder, so I know they are ready to capture my reaction to whatever jaw-dropper they are about to spring on me now.

"Ruthie," he starts, "the filming of the show didn't go at all like we had anticipated."

I nod in response, figuring that no one could have predicted how the twists and turns of the show would play out––even though the producers created much of the drama.

"I feel like you got the short end of the stick," he informs me, clearly trying to sound like he has empathy for me, even though I know that snakes aren't capable of conjuring that particular emotion.

"After discussing it with the other producers, we would like to offer you another chance to win the money. Afterall, you are one of the original cast members, and you won over the viewers with your choice of seemingly true love over cash."

I don't appreciate his use of the word 'seemingly.' It had been––and still is––true love on my side. It's not my fault if Andrew only pretended to reciprocate. It is amusing that I have now won over the viewers, though. I can see now that fame is a fickle thing with opinions flip-flopping from hate to love––and probably back again––at the drop of a hat.

I'm surprised to find that stardom is no longer important to me. Ironically, now that I have won over the audience, I no longer care what they think. Having millions of fans doesn't help a bit with the important things in life...like love and friendship and family.

T.J. continues on as if I am not having these enormous epiphanies about what truly matters to me. "So, we are prepared to double the financial incentive. We'll give you $500,000 to choose the money."

I stare at him dumbfounded. It should be tempting to accept, given that Andrew had been deceptive with me. That is a ton of money. It would set me up for life. Granted, it would be a life without Andrew, but I'm going to be without him anyway. *The choice should be simple...be poor and live without Andrew or be rich and live without Andrew...Duh. That's a no-brainer.*

It must look like I haven't comprehended what T.J. has offered because he decides to spell it out more clearly for me. "That's half a million dollars. The only thing you have to do to get the money is agree not to ever see Andrew Stark again."

"I...I...I...can't take the money."

I hear Baggy's exasperated sigh as she throws her arms up in the air. "Haven't I taught you anything?" she asks me.

T.J. turns to face the camera directly. "Well, there you have it, folks. True love does exist. Who would have thought?" He shrugs his shoulders like he just can't comprehend it.

"Ruthie has just chosen love over money, even though Andrew deceived her. It was an incredibly bold choice that I wouldn't have believed possible if I hadn't seen it with my own eyes."

I feel dumb for putting my feelings ahead of simple, unadulterated greed. The others in the room are clearly shocked over my choice. I can only imagine what the rest of the world will think when this video streams over the internet. Logically, I know that my choice doesn't make sense. If I'm going to be without Andrew anyway, why not drown my sorrows in a big pile of cash? I just couldn't take the money. It seemed like it would be a betrayal of my feelings, even if they aren't reciprocated.

"Last chance, Ruthie," T.J. seems determined to make me change my mind. "You want to walk away from this show empty-handed?"

I pause, trying to convince myself to accept the offer. Sensing my hesitation, T.J. adds, "I'll give you the cash right now." He opens a briefcase filled with neatly stacked bills that look like they were freshly printed, and I nearly stagger at the sight of it. It's more money than I have ever seen in one place in my entire lifetime. It looks like a bribe from a television crime show, except this is real money being offered to me, and I don't really have to do anything to take it.

Except, I would have to do something to take it––something monumental. I would have to deny my feelings for Andrew, like they aren't real. It would be like saying he doesn't matter to me. But he does matter to me. Despite his betrayal, he still matters very much to me. I can't deny that. I won't deny that.

I look straight into the croc's eyes and firmly say, "I choose love."

"You surprise me, Ruthie," Croc says before adding, "And so did Andrew. Bring him in," he mutters into his mike, shaking his head as if he's completely perplexed. Turning to face the camera, he says, "You saw it here, folks. Love wins out over money. These two lovebirds have both chosen each other over a great deal of money. Then, they chose each other again over double that amount of money."

My mind is trying to comprehend what T.J. has just said. *Andrew chose me over the money? Andrew chose me over the money?!? Twice?* It feels way too good to be true. My ears must be playing tricks on me—hearing only what they want to hear.

When Andrew appears in my doorway, it almost takes my breath away. "You chose me over the money?" he asks me, seeming genuinely surprised. "Again?" he croaks out the question, still standing by the door.

"Of course," I confirm, taken aback that he would doubt my feelings. After all, the only thing I kept secret from him was how long I carried a torch for him. He, however, hadn't bothered to tell me that the producers had arranged for him to be on the show to try to build some melodrama for me with my newlywed husband.

Considering that, I feel like I am the one who has the right to be shocked that he opted for me, when he had clearly been there for the money. "You chose me over that huge sum of cash?" I ask him, the first flicker of hope starting to flare deep in my belly.

He walks over to me then. "Of course," he tells me as if I should never have doubted him.

"And again when they doubled the prize?" My mind is working to muddle through and get caught up on everything that has happened.

"I did," he confirms, reaching out to tenderly rub the back of his finger along my jawline. "And I would no matter how many times they double it," he adds sweetly.

My glimmer of hope is beginning to burn much more brightly, but I still have questions. "You were planted there by the producers to seduce me," I accuse.

"I was," he admits, "but Ruthie, you have to believe me, I never intended to hurt you. Once we were reunited, I started to remember how being around you makes me feel. You were so familiar––your bubbling and contagious laughter, the way you tuck your hair behind your ears when you're nervous, the way your eyes light up when you see me, making me believe that I truly matter––yet you were different, more grown-up, more guarded, even more beautiful."

"Are you getting all of this?" T.J. interrupts the wonderful moment by asking Jake if he's rolling. At Jake's nod, T.J. enthuses, "This lovey-dovey mumbo-jumbo is going to translate into ratings gold!"

I take a moment to glare at T.J. for being so crass, but decide he is a lost cause. When Andrew begins speaking again, I turn my full attention back to him.

"Ruthie, I hate to admit it, but I came on the show for the money. My grandmother needs 24-hour care, and my family doesn't have the money to afford it. My mother has been doing her best, but she's worn out and she's not a trained caretaker. Grandma refuses to go to the nursing home."

"I'm familiar with the stubborn-as-a-mule grandmother problem." I turn to look at mine.

"Who me?" Baggy asks as if she is the most innocent and easy-going person around. When I don't respond to her, she turns to Jake, "Is she talking about me?" He shrugs, clearly not wanting to get into the middle of this minefield.

"So, you need the money for your family." I process this tidbit of information. "But you didn't take it. What will your mother and grandmother do?" I'm concerned that our feelings for each other have hindered his ability to financially help his family.

"We'll figure out another way to get the money," he promises. He seems so confident that I believe him. "The money isn't what is important. You are what is important."

Unable to hold back any longer, I rush into his arms for a long, sweet kiss. It feels like coming home being in his arms, and I savor the feeling of his warm embrace. "I was afraid I had lost you," I admit.

"Never," he says adamantly before adding, "I thought I lost you. I've never been so scared. I know it's not logical after so little time together, but I have incredibly strong feelings for you, Ruthie--stronger feelings than I've ever had for anyone else."

"Me too," I tell him as I go up on my tippy toes to kiss him again.

I forget all about the camera and the others in the room as we celebrate our reunion by making out. His kisses leave me breathless as our tongues explore each other's mouths.

"Welp," Baggy says loudly, "I guess the rest of us better get going, unless you're planning to record their reunion banging session?"

She asks the question of T.J., who seems utterly surprised by her saucy outspokenness. "Oh, umm, no. We have the footage we need, so we'll be heading out."

"Yeah, staying another five minutes would make the show take a completely different turn, wouldn't it?" Baggy seems to mull this over before adding, "Although, I bet you'd have plenty of viewers for that too."

Not wanting Baggy to give the sly producer any further ideas, I force myself to break our kiss. "Yes, you need to go. ALL of you." I look at Baggy for the second sentence. I wouldn't put it past her to see nothing wrong with hanging out while Andrew and I take our reunion celebration to the bedroom.

"Suit yourself," Baggy says, shrugging her shoulders and grabbing her belongings. "I need to get back to my hunky hubby anyway. He's probably been missing getting all up in this." She waves her hands up and down her scrawny body.

We can't seem to do anything but stare at her. We're likely all trying unsuccessfully to unsee the mental image she has just created. Not seeming to notice, Baggy heads for the door and holds it open for the others.

Shaking himself out of his wide-eyed stare, T.J. asks Baggy, "Have you ever considered doing reality television? The world deserves to get to know you." He hands her one of his thick business cards.

"Ohh," Baggy pats her chest, obviously flattered. "I'd love to." As she is closing the door behind them, I hear her ask him, "Have you considered a show about the inside scoop on a spy's life? I'm a super secret spy, you know."

We chuckle once the door closes. "She's one-of-a-kind," I grin at Andrew.

"Definitely," Andrew agrees before adding, "as are you."

"So, what now?" I ask him, feeling a little uncertain about how to move forward.

"Now we spend the night getting reacquainted with each other," he tells me.

I like the sound of spending the night with him, but I'm a little disappointed to not have more of a plan beyond the next twenty-four hours. Since we each gave up half a million dollars for the other one, I assumed we'd have more of a future together than one night between the sheets.

ANN OMASTA

Almost as if he can read my thoughts, Andrew continues, "And after tonight, we spend tomorrow night together and the night after that." He smiles down at me. "Until the nights blend into weeks, and the weeks turn into months, and the months become years. I hope we carry on that way, until we are old and gray horny toads like Baggy and her husband."

Laughter bubbles out of me at his accurate, but ornery description of my wild, wonderful grandmother. "We should be so lucky," I tell him.

"We will be so lucky," he promises. "I was dumb enough to let you slip away from me when we were teenagers, and I almost lost you again on that stupid cruise ship. I'm going to do everything in my power to make sure I never lose you again. I'm all in with us, Ruthie."

I think about how long I've been all in with Andrew––as long as I can remember. The actual man is even better than the one I imagined so many times over the years. I pull back to gaze up at him. "I'm SO all in with us," I tell him honestly.

The most adorable crinkles appear at the sides of his eyes as he teases me, "Always trying to one-up me." He kisses my nose before turning serious and saying, "I'm in love with you." Just as I'm gearing up to respond, he holds up a finger saying, "Don't even try to say you are MORE in love with me because it isn't possible."

"Okay," I smile up at him. "I am the MOST in love with you."

He's chuckling at my antics when I take his hand to lead him to my bedroom so we can start enjoying our perfect little slice of forever.

176

# EPILOGUE ~ A FEW MONTHS LATER

*I* can't believe we are engaged! Is it possible for a person to actually burst from excitement? If so, I might be in serious danger of it happening.

I think the only person more thrilled about my engagement is my sister, Roxy. She squealed so loud I had to hold the phone away from my ear after I told her. My mother had wrinkled her nose and looked down her glasses at Andrew when we told my parents the news. She did manage to give him a stiff hug, so there is hope that she will eventually come around. My affable father shook Andrew's hand and remained quiet, as he usually does.

Baggy will be thrilled by the news. She doesn't yet know because she hasn't called to check in lately, and she's not answering her cell phone. I'm not worried about her safety because it's not unusual for her to misplace her phone or forget to charge it. Besides, all of her big, dangerous spy talk is just talk––I think.

Andrew has moved into my place. He hadn't been enjoying doing the same tired show over and over for a luke-warm audience in Vegas every night. Before the producers approached him about the reality show, he had been considering moving back to our hometown to spend more time with his family anyway.

This tidbit makes me wonder if we would have run into each other and fallen in love, even without the nudge--okay, shove--from the show's producers. I'm guessing that we would have. We were obviously destined for each other. It just took Andrew a few years longer than me to realize it.

I smile to myself, thinking how he seems to be so incredibly happy with his work since he started his new business offering comedy magic shows for parties. He enjoys the more intimate setting that offers true interaction with his audiences. In the few short weeks since he started his new venture, he has already performed at several children's parties and now he has an adult-only version of his show ready to go for a bachelorette party next weekend.

Things are truly falling into place for us. That's why the out-of-the-blue phone call threw me for a bit of a loop.

I light a candle on our tiny dining room table, mulling over the conversation I just had and trying to determine how I feel about it. I'm not at all sure what Andrew's reaction will be when I tell him.

Evidently, I won't have to wait too long because I hear him close the door and hang up his keys. "Hi, Gorgeous," he beams at me before pulling me into a giant bear hug.

He pulls back to kiss me hungrily. I am tempted to move things to the bedroom before dinner like we usually end up doing. Tonight I need to talk to him, though, so I pull back to say, "Dinner's ready."

"Mmm, I'm starving and it smells delicious...almost as delicious as you."

We settle at the table with our plates piled high with spaghetti. "What's all this?" he asks me, indicating the wine and candle.

"Me trying to butter you up." I give him a mischievous grin.

"Uh oh," he teases me before turning serious and adding, "Anything for you. Just name it."

I like his open-ended acceptance of my mystery request, but I'm not sure if he'll feel as agreeable when he finds out what I want. I take a gulp of my white wine before telling him, "T.J. called me today."

His brow immediately furrows with distaste. "Ah, the jerkwad who tried to pay us not to be together."

"Yes, him," I smile at my fiancé. Deciding to start with flattery, I say, "It seems that the reality television world loves us and they want more of us."

Andrew drops his fork and looks at me like I have gone crazy. "I'm not doing some kind of newlyweds show where they follow us around and devise problems to try to split us up."

"Oh, no, I wouldn't do anything like that," I assure him.

"Are they sending us on another Cruise for Love?" he asks.

"We already found love," I remind him, but the enamored way he's looking at me makes it clear he already knows that. "Actually, they want us to get married in Las Vegas. They'll pay for the entire wedding AND give us $100,000!"

"What's the catch?" Andrew is very suspicious of anything related to Croc and his cohorts.

"They just want to film the wedding prep and our nuptials to stream for the world to see."

"A ready-made wedding video?" he smiles at me, and I sense that he is starting to warm to this idea, as I am...What is the harm? Why not? At my nod, he asks me, "Is this what you want?"

I consider the question. The show brought about major humiliation, heartache, and hurt feelings in me, but it also made it possible for me to reconnect with the man of my dreams. I shrug my shoulders, still not completely sure that this is a good idea, but excited about it nonetheless.

Making a snap decision, I say, "I'm in."

He studies me for a moment, his lids lowered. "If you're in, I'm in," he tells me. "Let's do this."

# BONUS EXCERPT FROM ISLAND HOPPING

I'm not overly surprised when I look out the window and see the naked, wrinkled, and saggy white butt pointed in my direction. Knowing this is just the woman's latest antic to try to get under my skin, I refuse to allow it to bother me.

After unlocking and raising my living room window, I yell outside through the screen, "Good morning, Baggy!"

Standing up to her full four feet, eight inches of height, with her pants still around her ankles, the spry little old lady turns around to glare at me. She's obviously disappointed that her prank didn't upset me.

Shaking my head, I decide the least I can do is play along with her ornery game. "That's a good one. You really got me this time, Baggy!"

At this the older woman beams and yanks her pants back up. Raising her fist in the air like she has just won a race, she toddles back down the road towards her house, without giving me another glance. Hopefully, that means she is done badgering me, at least for the rest of the day.

She has been trying for months to punish me for hurting her granddaughter, Roxy. I can't even get mad at the old lady's crazy shenanigans because I deserve whatever she dishes out in my direction.

Roxy is my best friend. *Or was.* We'd been best friends since our first day of preschool. The fact that I stole her fiancé, Gary, the night before her planned wedding to him still doesn't compute... even in my own mind. It is so far removed from everything I stand for. It's like I threw the whole 'sisters before misters' thing out the window for that brief moment in time. I can't believe I let that loser kiss me after their rehearsal dinner.

That ill-advised kiss set off a whirlwind of events, including Gary texting Roxy on the actual day of their planned nuptials to tell her the wedding was cancelled because he and I were in love.

The fact that he *texted* her with this information should have been a major clue to both of us that Gary was not a great catch. Telling her that he and I were in love because I made the mistake of letting him kiss me once is such a wildly preposterous leap that I almost wonder if the man is delusional.

He obviously was looking for any excuse to get out of marrying Roxy, but I wish with all my heart that I hadn't allowed myself to become his escape route.

The devastating turn of events actually worked out for the best for Roxy. She met the man of her dreams, which is obviously not Gary, and is now madly in love with the hunk from Hawaii. This positive outcome doesn't negate the fact that my betrayal was wrong. I would love to go back to that night and make it right. That's obviously not a possibility, so I'm focusing on doing everything in my power to make it up to Roxy and gracefully accepting whatever punishments her sister, Ruthie, and grandmother, Baggy, deem appropriate.

Roxy has, for the most part, forgiven me for the transgression. We'll probably never be as close as we once were, but she is taking the high road and working to move past the giant rift I created between us.

Ruthie and Baggy, however, are showing no signs of ever forgiving, forgetting, or moving on. Their persistent fury with me hurts a great deal because the two of them had always been like my adopted family.

Roxy and I were so close growing up, that I spent almost more time at the Rose household than I did my own. I had always considered Ruthie to be my pesky kid sister, since I didn't have any siblings of my own. Although we teased and picked on her, I loved her as fiercely and unconditionally as if she were my sister by blood.

Baggy was in a category of her own. As a toddler, Roxy's childish version of 'bad grandma' had come out of her tiny mouth sounding like Baggy. The moniker was so appropriate that it had stuck. Everyone called her Baggy, not just family. In fact, I have no idea what her given name is. She's simply Baggy, and it suits her to a tee.

My maternal grandmother passed away at an early age. Since my father bailed on my mother before I was born, I don't know my paternal grandparents at all. Baggy stepped in from the time I was about five to brilliantly and unconventionally fill that vital role in my life. Although she is often wildly inappropriate and outrageous, I love her with all my heart. It devastates me that she is so angry with me, even though I deserve it.

As I slice a banana for my oatmeal, I sigh and smile as I think about all the crazy things Baggy has done over the years. Her daughter, Caroline, Roxy and Ruthie's stuffy mother, is constantly yelling at Baggy to behave, as if the younger woman is the parent.

Once my teapot whistles, I pour the hot water into my oatmeal bowl and into my pre-warmed tea mug. Dunking the orange pekoe teabag in the hot water, I realize that tea is such a priority in my life because of Baggy. Whenever any of us girls were upset about something, she was always there with a warm mug of tea and a soft, reassuring hug.

I can feel the tears glistening in my eyes as I realize how much I miss having her sometimes bonkers, always soothing presence in my life. One stupid kiss had lost me a best friend, a sister, and a grandmother. Not to mention the fact that I am now a social pariah in our small town.

The Rose family is beloved by all, and I have managed to alienate them. Until it was gone, I didn't realize how much of my social standing came from being accepted as an unofficial member of their family.

Biting my lip as I rinse the blueberries for my hot cereal, I try for the thousandth time to think of a way to make it up to them. Roxy claims to have forgiven me, but I know she will never forget what I did. Our relationship will likely never get back to what it was before that life-ruining kiss. Besides, she lives in Hawaii now, so it's not like we can hang out on a daily basis.

Ruthie and Baggy view my betrayal of Roxy as a personal affront. They are showing no signs of ever getting over it, and I can't say that I blame them. I wouldn't be able to forgive someone for hurting my sweet, caring, and wonderful friend, either. In fact, I haven't forgiven myself, so why should I expect them to do so?

I eat my breakfast without really tasting it. The morning news program is on, but I can't focus on it. I'm such a fixer at work, it boggles my mind that I can't carry that talent over into my personal life and make things right with my three favorite ladies (other than my own mother, of course).

Speaking of my mom, I know she is ashamed of my transgression. She hasn't ever called me out on it, but I can tell that she is disappointed. Being seen with me in public has made her an outcast in town, too, and for that, I am truly sorry. I don't know what to do to make it up to her, other than to try to earn the forgiveness of Roxy's family.

Roxy and Ruthie's parents are civil whenever we bump into each other, but they are even more standoffish than they used to be. They never have been my biggest fans, but they permitted me to be absorbed into the folds of their family as an honored guest. I'm sure they feel betrayed by my mistake too.

The knock at my front door startles me out of my rumination as I rinse out my empty bowl and mug. After drying off my hands with the red and white kitchen towel that reads, *Kiss the Cook*, which Ruthie gave me as a housewarming gift when I bought this condo a few years ago, I head to answer it.

Already knowing who is probably on the other side and hoping to curb any more of her pranks for the day, I yell, "I have to finish getting ready for work, Baggy."

Wondering if she had simply 'ding-donged and dashed,' or if she had left me an unpleasant surprise, like a bag of flaming dog poop, I fling the door open.

"Oh!" I yell out in surprise at the slick-looking businessman on the other side of the door. Suddenly, I wish that I could be better about being a little more stringent with security, like peering through the peephole before opening my door to strangers.

"Expecting a batty old woman?" The man's exaggerated smile reveals an abundance of big, white teeth. It reminds me of a cartoon shark.

I am perplexed by how he knows Baggy and a little affronted by what he has called her. His description is perfectly accurate, but my hackles are raised nonetheless.

Feeling annoyed by his obvious arrogance, I snap, "I don't have time for uninvited guests. Whatever you're selling, I don't want."

My strong, negative reaction to this man surprises me, but I'm in too far to back down now. With a brisk nod, I soften my previous sentiment by adding, "Good day."

When I try to slam the door shut, he sticks his shiny leather, expensive-looking shoe in the opening to keep the door from fully closing.

I gape at him, stunned by his audacity. As he reaches into his pocket, my first thought is that he might be reaching for a weapon, so I am immediately relieved when he pulls out a business card.

Shoving the card through the opening his foot is demanding, I decide to accept it in the hope that he will then leave.

Glancing down at the thick card stock, I am surprised to see only one line of embossed lettering... 'T.J. Stone, Producer.'

**Start Island Hopping NOW!**

# REVIEWS ~ BEST. GIFT. EVER.

Now is the time to help other readers. Many people rely on reviews to make the decision about whether or not to get a book. You can help them make that decision by leaving your thoughts on what you found enjoyable about this book.

If you liked this book, please consider leaving a positive review. Even if it's just a few words, your input makes a difference and will be received with much gratitude.

# ABOUT THE AUTHOR - ANN OMASTA

Ann Omasta is a USA Today bestselling author.

Ann's Top Ten list of likes, dislikes, and oddities:

1. I despise whipped cream. There, I admitted it in writing. Let the ridiculing begin.

2. Even though I have lived as far south as Key Largo, Florida, and as far north as Maine, I landed in the middle.

3. If I don't make a conscious effort not to, I will drink nothing but tea morning, noon, and night. Hot tea, sweet tea, green tea--I love it all.

4. There doesn't seem to be much in life that is better than coming home to a couple of big dogs who are overjoyed to see me. My other family members usually show significantly less enthusiasm about my return.

5. Singing in my bestest, loudest voice does not make my family put on their happy faces. This includes the big, loving dogs referenced above.

6. Yes, I am aware that bestest is not a word.

7. Dorothy was right. There's no place like home.

8. All of the numerous bottles in my shower must be lined up with their labels facing out. It makes me feel a little like Julia Roberts' mean husband from the movie *Sleeping with the Enemy*, but I can't seem to control this particular quirk.

9. I love, love, love finding a great bargain!

10. Did I mention that I hate whipped cream? It makes my stomach churn to look at it, touch it, smell it, or even think about it. Great--now I'm thinking about it. Ick!

On a serious note, I hope that you enjoyed reading this book as much as I loved writing it!

# JOIN ANN'S CLAN!

Are you a SUPER FAN of Ann's? Do you LOVE Ann's books? Do you READ all of Ann's books and leave REVIEWS? Do you like SHARING great books with your friends? If so, send an email message to Ann (author@annomasta.com) to see if there is a spot available in her group: **ANN's CLAN**.

**What's in it for you?** You'll get Advance Review Copies (ARCs) of Ann's hot new releases, insider info, special giveaways, personal interaction with one of your favorite authors, and tons of other fun stuff. As a member of Ann's Clan, you might get to name a character in one of Ann's books, help choose a title, or vote on a book's cover. The possibilities are endless! Email now to see if there is an opening in **Ann's Clan**.

# COPYRIGHT